MASTER
OF RODS AND STRINGS

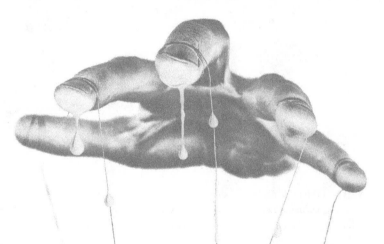

Jason Marc Harris

MW00436384

MASTER OF RODS AND STRINGS

Copyright 2021 by Jason Marc Harris

All rights reserved

No part of this book may be reproduced in any form or any electronic or mechanical means, including information and retrieval storage systems, without written permission from the author, except for the use of brief quotations in a book review.

Cover art and design © 2021 by Sean Leddy Creative
Design and interior by ElfElm Publishing

Available as a trade paperback, hardcover, and eBook from Vernacular Books.

ISBN (TPB) 978-1-952283-15-4

ISBN (eBook) 978-1-952283-14-7

Visit us online at VernacularBooks.com

To Marjorie Belle Miller & Stephen LeRoy Harris,
both of whom exited the fretful stage of rods and strings
all too soon; to Kevin Lee Harris, whose life strings
were severed by the worst sort of blood alchemy, and to
Geoffrey Edwin Harris, who has moved like Elias once
did to the sea, where hopefully surprising if not uncanny
guidance and companionship awaits.

And to Vickie Harris, Isaac Harris, and Amaya Harris—
all for whom even the weirdest tales are woven with love.

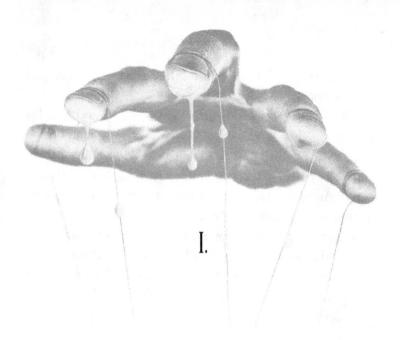

I.

I WILL NOT DENY THAT I HAVE ALWAYS BEEN FASCINATED WITH puppets.

Perhaps because I was born on a farm in Saint Siméon, a forgotten town west of Valence in southern France named after the patron saint of puppets. Despite the frequent puppet shows—many families considered themselves extraordinarily lucky if a child were accepted into the Lycée Avancé des Marionettes to study such puppetry—not all were enthusiastic. Neither my father, Patrick Clermont, nor my mother, Anne Belleau, ever bought me a puppet.

I sulked over this injustice. At the age of four, I could only watch my sister, Sonja, play with Angélique, a fairy marionette with long red hair that our Uncle Pavan had bought her.

Occasionally, when she noticed me moping, Sonja would let me pull at the strings. Although I could get Angélique to do a flopping walk, I never could make her glide gracefully as my sister did. Sonja's twirling flourishes of thumbs and rippling fingers gave Angélique life.

"Such talent, such polish." Uncle Pavan rubbed his thumbs together as he watched Angélique slide amid potted plants in the garden and float up to the doll's house to join Sonja. She played at the strings like a harp by whose invisible sounds Angélique moved with buoyant grace, almost hovering at times, as if her delicate azure wings could truly fly.

Uncle Pavan's own prowess at puppetry was marvelous. Some whispered he could literally bring puppets to life. He took a dedicated interest in Sonja's future. That is why I have so few memories of her. She left for the advanced arts of puppetry.

I was left alone.

I longed to play with Sonja as we had on brighter days of jumping on piles of autumn leaves or racing through fields with the spring winds—chasing harvest mice and Swallowtail butterflies between stalks of shuddering wheat or corn. When I brooded and stroked Sebastian, our silky-furred black cat, who had also been the playmate of Sonja, I decided that if I showed myself particularly adept at puppets like my sister, then I would be reunited with her.

Despite Father's refusal to buy me a marionette—though I bawled for one during walks down cobblestone streets in the marketplace of Saint-Siméon—Uncle Pavan, who was half-Italian, brought back from a summer trip to Italy one of its most famous puppets, Gianduja. Uncle Pavan's passion for puppetry extended to his purse strings. He spent much wealth to sponsor children to master the art of rods and strings.

As Uncle made Gianduja bend and hop about with herky-jerky motion, I laughed.

My father scowled but then accompanied Gianduja's antics with violin.

Once I began dancing, Father smiled.

"Look, Elias loves to dance with music," he told Mother, who smiled thinly back at him.

But it was not the music that made me laugh, jump, and frolic. It was the puppet.

This new marionette looked sharp in his black coat with red fringes, and the Ferrari family (most famous of Italian puppeteer-dynasties) had added dark blue trim to the red-and-black tricorne hat that sat upon the puppet's frowning and sour face. That red-button-eyed grimace made the mannequin look like he must be about to speak.

And speak he did, though only in my dreams since Uncle took Giandjuja away with him.

"I can show you how to really play the violin," the diminutive Gianduja mouthed at me in a dream upon a beach of black sand beneath red lights that spiraled into an indigo sky.

Play we did. Together we sawed and wailed across a stage where insect-headed people chirped, and countless puppets of every shape and size and color hummed and sang. Before sleep, I imagined the nightly concerts—I'd stare at my bedroom wall, which would shiver with grainy but vivid phantasmagoria.

Two years later when my father, stooped of back and calloused of chin, proposed to teach me the violin in waking life, he was astonished to find my uncanny facility with the bow.

"Gianduja plays even better than you, Papa. He shows me how at night."

Father gently adjusted my right arm. "Ah, but he does not hold the bow properly."

My improper posture continued to vex my father, but he was always patient with me because of my impeccable sense of rhythm and my powerful feelings that occasionally surfaced in a rousing crescendo or heartbreaking diminuendo.

I remember one day as I pined for Sonja, he told me to use my melancholy on the strings. "You are already good, but you can be a great musical performer, my boy! You must harness your passions. Now, that elbow, keep it under the violin. Yes, better, better. Ah, you make each note sing."

"It's as though the boy feels the strings right up his bones, into his ribs and heart," Father told Mother, who didn't look over at our practice sessions while she sewed up a ripped cravat for one of her few clients.

She pressed her thin lips together. "Let the boy be what he is. No more no less."

"So you said about his sister." Father's smile collapsed into drooping marionette lines.

Mother did not even glance at his crumpled face. She stared out the window at the corn and wheat bending beneath the evening breeze and the setting sun.

We had not seen Sonja in six months. Father explained that this was no mystery, but the result of her prodigy. Since Uncle Pavan had remarked her facility with puppets four years ago, and as a star pupil of rod and string, she worked tirelessly at puppetry. She was free from the daily struggle between dirt and shoot, thread and seam.

I listened to Sebastian's purrs for some inkling of when his mistress would return, but he at least seemed content to wait. The first snow would be coming, and my heart beat in a frenzy of disappointment as I feared that my sister would not join me in building a snowman.

She did not come home for Christmas or Easter. With cowards' eyes, my parents evaded my questions about when she would return, putting me off, month by month. No gifts could replace what they'd stolen.

In May, the flower petals blew. Alone, I chased after them. Only breezes caressed me.

Meanwhile, Father, who practiced more than ever—baggy eyes redder from sleepless nights—still attempted to make a musical genius of me, but he observed with disappointment and pique that I preferred make-believe with invisible puppets rather than work with the violin. Sure of foot, I liked jigging about to the music rather than performing it. And when I played the violin, I pretended Gianduja and his grand puppet audience delighted to watch me.

Walking home from school through Saint Siméon's narrow streets, I'd gaze with longing at grinning and pouting faces that looked out from puppet shops. Once a month, the Carnivaux des Marionettes played in town, and I'd sneak away to watch and wonder at how their handlers could perform such miracles of movement.

I also shadowed local daily street shows.

One of the street puppeteers, named Yves, was amused by my devotion. He gave me a memorable lesson there among the dark blur of gray cobblestones.

"The life of puppets," he said, untwisting the strings of his marionette menagerie, "is the dance of the fingers. Puppeteers of old—they say—would connect wires from their veins, feeding lifeblood to puppets to entice the spirits of the earth to enter them. Today, we do this with strings. You move, like so, and he moves. A thing is dead until it moves. You bring it life."

I listened to his macabre words and wondered if he meant to scare me with this tale of bloodthirsty puppeteers. I was far from afraid. In fact, I longed to enter into that secret communion with puppets like those marvels of the legendary past.

Yves twitched his knuckles. The horse marionette rose and clip-clopped across the road.

After a half-hour of imitating Yves, I began to get the trick of it.

Yves clicked his tongue. "You could be something one day. You must keep at it."

One night after the full moon bloomed yellow over our blotchy and stunted wheat stalks, Uncle Pavan brought Sonja for a visit after her twelfth birthday. She did not join me in racing through our miserable crop. She preferred to sit on the couch with Sebastian.

Sonja petted the cat while listening to Father play the violin. After rushing through Debussy, Father set down the instrument and bemoaned the moldy winter wheat which had followed this summer's blighted corn.

I asked Sonja to show me what she had learned of puppets.

"I didn't bring one, my dear little cabbage," Sonja said. She smiled, but sadly. Her slate gray eyes did not flash with the spark I'd seen in our childhood games.

"Never fear, my children," Uncle Pavan boomed. From his billowing overcoat he drew out the fairy dancer, Angélique, with which Sonja had demonstrated her virtuosity years ago. Those butterfly wings flashed azure, and Angélique's eyes shone orange with speckled topaz. Her red hair complemented her violet dress, but I noticed the front of her head now had silvery-blond bangs that matched my sister's own hair color.

This similarity made me long to stroke that puppet's hair, to make friends, maybe even to kiss this strange cousin or little sister of my own.

I looked at my family to see if they shared in my delight at seeing Angélique, but my sister's face tightened, and my parents looked away. Uncle Pavan stared at me, not Sonja. He pulled forward the diminutive butterscotch hand of the puppet and pinched one of my blond locks, which my mother had let grow long—hating to cut them, she said. I winced at the stinging tug on my scalp. Angélique's topaz eyes looked at me, almost cruelly, I thought. Uncle Pavan released me and I saw how in one quick movement Angélique's delicate palm brushed against his own large free hand. "So many gifts with this boy."

Sebastian, swishing his tail stiffly back-and-forth, watched the proceeding warily from his bed of straw in the corner of the dining room.

"Angélique needs a dance partner," Uncle Pavan said. "Pick up the strings, my talented boy."

I brushed my rumpled hair across my forehead then took hold of the perch that guided the marionette. I gyrated my wrist to flap Angélique's fairy wings, but I pulled the strings too hard. Angélique toppled over, startling Sebastian, who sprang up to the kitchen window and leapt out.

"You see? Elias is not one for the puppets," Father snapped. Whether directed at me, Mother, or Uncle Pavan I could not tell, but shame and anguish boiled inside my chest.

Uncle Pavan looked at me and slowly pulled at his mustache. I began to cry.

"Maybe not. Or maybe . . . not yet," he rumbled. "Let's see him with the fiddle then."

Sonja patted me on the back and whispered, "It is far better not to be for the puppets."

I bit my quivering lip and blinked back tears of wounded pride.

Father shoved the violin at me. I played a dispirited march. A half-step out of time. By the time I finished, Uncle Pavan had drunk half the bottle of wine, had stopped touching his mustache, and clapped cheerfully.

Father did not clap. His jaw clenched and bulged.

Mother refilled Uncle Pavan's glass, then her own, and avoided looking at both her husband and Uncle Pavan.

"Sonja," Uncle Pavan said, his ruddy bald head gleaming with a glaze of sweat, "let us see Angélique dance—truly."

With her face dipped in shadows of the flickering lantern, Sonja bit at her thumbs, then picked up Angélique's perch. Without even bothering to unwind the strings, she whisked her fingers in an elegant curl while drawing up her wrist. In a rippling pirouette, Angélique rose and spun about the center of the room.

My tears dried as I stared at my sister, so magical and wonderful. An actual fairy herself.

While Sonja's fingers spun like a spider cocooning a hapless fly, Angélique performed a gliding, acrobatic, and mesmerizing waltz. Sonja's own feet slid quietly over the floor. She wore flat black ballet shoes that Uncle Pavan must have purchased to help her technique be flawless.

When Sonja had finished, Uncle Pavan bellowed, "Isn't she tremendous?"

Father and Mother stayed quiet.

Sonja looked at her black shoes. Why had she come home so glum?

"I have worked so long on that dance, it would be a wonder if it weren't pleasing."

"Ever so modest and practical," Uncle Pavan said. "But you see, she is ready to tour. Talent such as hers should not be for Saint Siméon alone."

Father opened his mouth to speak, but did not say a word when Mother pointed at Sonja.

"You're bleeding," Mother said.

"Just my thumbs." Sonja sucked at one, then the other. Angélique's perch also had flecks of blood from where Sonja's bitten thumb oozed on the polished wood.

"No." Mother pointed to the back of Sonja's dress, the red splotch that soaked from her groin down her leggings.

Sonja's eyes were watery and her face blanched when she rushed to the bathroom, paling like a ghost nearing its dawn dissolution. Mother followed her.

The rest of us waited till Mother and my sister reappeared. Still pale, she looked down at her flat ballet shoes as if some secret answer lay between them.

Mother frowned. "Please, you must keep her better. Sonja is not a little girl anymore."

"No," Uncle Pavan said, his broad thumbs stroking the base of his chin. "She is not."

"And you've come to take her even further away from us? Can she not at least visit more frequently?" Father's blood-shot eyes glared at my jovial Uncle.

Pavan, hands folded behind his back as he paced the room, spoke as if lecturing to an audience at the theater or advising an official committee. "Although her early childhood was enriched by the wholesome earth, farmlife does not permit full dedication to the art. Her fingers would lose their subtle feel of string and rods. Tutors from all over the world work at our school, and Sonja is their most prized pupil. As she is mine. It is no exaggeration to say that young Sonja and her puppets will achieve truly unique greatness."

My chest swelled in pride for Sonja, but also poignant jealousy and longing at not yet being able to join her. I missed her terribly, and I craved "truly unique greatness" too.

But why did Father's hands shake, and Mother knit more furiously, while Uncle spoke?

Father stretched his lips in a wan smile. "Noble of you to take such interest in her career."

Pavan stopped pacing. He held our Father's gaze. "It is a good month before her first tour. A monumental step in her progress. To fully prepare her, I will teach her all that I know of the grand arts of puppetry."

"All that you know." Gnarling his chapped fingers into claws, Father shut his eyes.

Uncle Pavan looked away from Father's strangeness and out at the failed crops crackling in the evening wind. "Could you keep two children, with a year like this, for the farm?"

Father opened his eyes but said nothing. A husk of himself brought in from dry fields.

Uncle Pavan hummed, stepped over to me. He ruffled my hair with his broad hands.

"Such beautiful hair. The marvel of the golden fleece here in this age of steam and steel."

He drew out a scissors and cut a lock of my hair. The same one I think that Angélique had pinched. He stuffed the sheared lock into his inner coat pocket.

"Something to remember my nephew by." He patted his coat like he'd stolen a big secret.

Outside, a cat screeched in pain. I rushed outdoors to see Sebastian attempting to drag himself up the steps to the porch. His left leg was bloodied and missing half his furry toes.

As I wrapped Sebastian in a towel, my family came out and saw the disaster.

"Oh no, Sebastian!" Sonja cried. She kneeled to stroke his quivering, blood-speckled ears.

"It's one of those overgrown foxes that did this." Father growled and clawed at his ribs.

Uncle Pavan watched me pet poor Sebastian. Then he pulled out Gianduja from his coat.

Why did Sonja duck as if dodging a wasp? Jealous that I finally received my own puppet present?

Uncle Pavan set Gianduja on a wicker chair. "Gianduja, I trust, will be of some comfort."

As Sebastian yowled his final wails of anger, pain, and fear to the mucous-colored moon, Father did not object that I had something to cling to.

The house was no home after Sonja's departure, which felt like a second death following so soon after the lethal mauling of Sebastian. Because Father set traps for rats that invaded our farm now that Sebastian's watch had ended, I became accustomed to the bodies of dead rodents.

I puzzled over the mystery that separated the twitch of life from the stiffness of death.

When I played violin, I composed songs in D-minor that were somber and dissonant. My father wrinkled his nose at the disconcerting melodies, reminding me that I still had much to learn before I became a true musician. His guidance irritated me. And made me more morose.

Playing with Gianduja did not distract me much from the

knowledge that he too was a dead thing, no matter what Yves had told me of how the strings could dance a puppet to life.

However, that old macabre notion of the puppet's dance of blood still intrigued me. I thought of Sebastian's still-fresh corpse buried in the corner of the carrot field beneath the columnar poplar tree. Wires, Yves had said, ran the lifeblood from the puppeteer's veins to his avatars of cloth and strings. Had Sonja's bitten and bleeding thumbs helped Angélique dance?

The violin lessons, not surprisingly, were doomed to come to an end.

When Father roared through the house upon discovering his polished mahogany instrument stripped of its visceral strings, the last thing he might have suspected was that I had attached those strings to poor Sebastian, to whom I tried to give back life by pinching the strings between my bleeding thumbs, moving each paw, one-at-a-time, a step closer to the milk dish. But even though I pricked my thumbs first with Mother's sewing pins, so they bled at least as much as I had seen Sonja's, it was no good. I had heard Father refer to the strings as "threads of cat gut," but I always thought that was an expression referring to how the violin sometimes whined like a feline.

Years later, I would reflect on my failure at reanimating-puppetry. I would consider that because the violin strings were not conductive metal, but mere cat gut after all, that they could not transmit the electric pulse of life. Dead cannot bring back dead.

My wretchedness at my technical failure was com-pounded by the shock of what Father did next.

After staring in amazement at how I had attached myself to Sebastian, he cursed and called me a "Monster." Father pulled away the reddened violin strings, seized Sebastian by his tail and swung him through the window.

Poor Sebastian catapulted out into the muddy field.

As I cowered and clutched at Gianduja for support, Father tore the puppet from my arms. He yanked apart each of his dangling legs and, crushing the torso and head between his calloused hands, hurled the only thing left I thought I could rely on out into that dark night.

His voice rasped horribly. "There! Let that be an end of such damned foolishness!"

"If it were only so easy," Mother said. She shook her head at my father. "Didn't you see, how he took the boy's hair?"

Instead of rising to comfort me, as I bawled like an infant buried alive, Mother's lips pressed together, and she kept knitting a sweater of red triangles and blue, olive-like eyes.

I ran outside. Tears mixed with bloated drops of rain and slid past my eyebrows down my sniffling nose.

Clouds flickered with skinny veins of chalk-white lightning as I staggered into the field of withered stalks and fell to the mushy ground.

A ripping report of thunder crashed as I got back up from the clench of thick muck.

I squished around the perimeter of the field and found Sebastian, his body twisted into a matted mess of fur, his protruding tongue rough against my grasping fingers. My thumbs stung as I stroked his fur, pinching between the grooves of his clawed paws. Sniveling, I wiped my nose and pressed my cheeks to his whiskers, hugged the still cuddly texture that covered the wet frame of bone and sinew. Feeling his stiffness, I howled at the strobing flashes of storm and squeezed my fists till nails bit past soil, grit. Both hands bled.

And then, as I paused in the dry heaves of my affliction, I saw the glint of crimson eyes.

Gianduja looked upon me.

His back was supported against one of the wooden stakes propping up an overripe tomato plant—its rusty dry-rotted fruit blighted by grubs and drought. Gianduja appeared almost serene despite missing his legs. I crawled towards him and cut my right hand on a sharp rock near the base of the stake. As I hissed and raised my hand, the blood dribbled onto Gianduja's sagging face, mildew-scented already from the pervasive dampness. I patted his filthy tricorne hat and winced at the sensitivity my recent injury had awakened.

"Elias!"

My parents stood in the doorway. They searched for me in the raging storm. It was Father who called out, but Mother walked with him into the veil of rain and blast of wind.

I lay numb, watching Gianduja and rubbing my fingertips against my bloodied thumbs. In the whip of wet gusts, I saw Gianduja's head dip to the left, as though he were curious about my plight. And when I felt myself lifted by my parents, carrying me like some funereal burden or sacred cargo—losing weight and gravity as though preparing to float up into the blurry sky—I glanced back towards the receding line of ruined crops, and I knew I saw Gianduja's placid face quiver into a smile. Those glassy red eyes stared after me— not with the fellowship that I longed for, nor the malice that I feared I recognized—but with an appetite for that which I did not yet understand.

A week later, we were leaving Saint Siméon and moving to Marseille. No, we couldn't wait until the end of summer.

No, we didn't have time to say goodbye to Sonja. We had to move now. Mother gave me a sewing kit and demanded I wear the sweater she'd knit with the blue staring eyes and red triangles. A traditional design her Gypsy grandmother had taught her. Mother said it would keep me safe from malicious glares. I told her it was not Halloween, and witches would not be out with their evil eyes. She shook her head and explained there are "other things in the world that can bear down on a boy," make him a helpless slave to a malign will.

"A compliment from a false heart," she said, "has more deadly venom than an insult from a proclaimed enemy."

To humor her, I took the sweater. And I packed up the kit of needle and thread as well, for I did not sneer at the essential craft of sewing, which I recognized as an asset to shaping, stitching, and costuming puppets that would one day be my prized companions.

I could not understand these forces that pulled at me from the world beyond. How was it that Sebastian and Sonja should be taken away, and I should have to leave the very house where I had grown up with the wheat and corn and my darling sister?

The only thing I did not regret was losing Gianduja. He had become repellent with his uncanny smile leering from the ruined harvest. I puzzled over that smile among the rotting tomatoes. I could not explain the meaning of what I'd witnessed. And I resented having any secret kept from me. Was all that I saw only a bad waking dream?

It was not the only dream I wondered about. I had several dreams about what might lie within Uncle Pavan's home and lurk at his school. Dancing puppets, tasty feasts, and wild strange celebrations.

Before leaving, I tried to see Sonja at her school.

I gazed with longing at the boys and girls in every room either engaged in the design or craft of puppetry. Peering through the first open door, I saw a group of children fashioning a scarf puppet. Scarlet and indigo threads flashed while slender fingers and narrow wrists measured and cut cloth. In another room, where I heard girls' tinny clinks of laughter, I dared to open the door. Standing in the center of the room, a giant spider puppet with an old woman's crinkly face swerved on peg-like stalks. From beneath the ridges of the thick rubbery body, curls of brown-haired girls emerged, giggling in trills when they saw me staring.

"Is Sonja here?" I asked from room to room. At last, one older girl wearing a silver beret told me Sonja was "on a special trip with Master Pavan." She said she did not know where.

Hearing these discouraging words, my face crumpled, my lower lip quaked, and I blinked back as best I could the surge of warm tears.

One tall boy, whose two-headed owl puppet fluttered in the hallway, laughed at me. The wings of his owl flapped above my head, and its sharp talons clutched at my shoulders while the boy hooted, "Who-who, oh who are you? Why you going boo-hoo-who?"

This taunting and frightful attack—performed with an enviable dexterity I did not yet possess—combined with my frustration and grief at not seeing my sister, drove me into paralysis. I huddled against the wall, covering my defeated eyes with my hands.

"Let him alone, Desmond," the older girl said. "He's Sonja's little brother."

Desmond's dark eyes narrowed. Both heads of the owl-puppet swiveled to regard me.

"So what? He's not a student here. He's not good enough to get in. He's a nobody!"

One of the owl-beaks nibbled at the ends of my fleecy bangs until I batted the puppet away. I looked up at this smirking spiky-haired tormentor, and my blurry eyes cleared. Despite Desmond's scary assault with his baleful bird, now that I had calmed down, I was not quite so impressed with his showy puppetry. Nor was he ready to fight. His hands were hidden in the sheath of the owl-puppet, one hand controlling each head, which bobbed simultaneously at me.

I rushed forward and hit him in the gut. Still smirking, he staggered back and glared.

"I'll teach you who the nobody is!" I screamed, a loud voice from a small boy.

"Stop this!" The girl barged between us, her silver beret glistening over her smooth hair.

I hurried away before Desmond could hit me back. I had no doubt he could hit harder than me, but Desmond never withdrew his hands from his puppet. Instead, he hooted and those damned bird heads turned and turned, yellow eyes watching, wings flapping, talons twitching.

"You're a nobody! And your sister? She's a whore!"

I clenched my fists and fled the halls of that school.

The words burned as I made my way into the cobblestone lanes. How could he say such things? Why did God let horrible kids be chosen above me? Why had Uncle Pavan taken Sonja away on this "special" trip?

I muttered prayers to St. Siméon for guidance. For a reunion with my sister.

In sullen despair and stung pride, I wandered through the streets. A lost soul.

At last, I resolved to go to Uncle Pavan's home, hoping to find further clues about Sonja.

I saw motion and light within his mansion on the East side of town by the river. Had Uncle Pavan returned already from the trip? At last I would discover what secrets Uncle hid.

From an immense yew tree that flanked one side of his house, I peered through a window. Uncle sat in a robe of what looked like scarlet silk before the fireplace.

He dangled a marionette in one hand and gripped Sonja's wrist with the other. I could not see my sister's face to see if she might be suffering or what exactly my Uncle was doing with her. I edged along the yew's thick branch and stepped onto the parapet, so I could see better.

Something hung from strings near the fireplace. Gianduja. Still dirty, and his red eyes had been torn out. Yet, I still felt the living gaze of the vacant sockets upon me. I shivered.

As orange flames blurred and waved in the fireplace, Uncle Pavan, now bare-chested but colored with jagged inky angles of arcane etchings in his flesh, pulled at the strings of the dancer, Angélique, shining with starry specks hanging from her cottony hair.

Then Angélique stepped forward and seemed to dance by herself. A chill ran through me.

My sister pulled away from Uncle Pavan, but she did not run or scream.

She stared at the glamorous puppet. Then, one of its dainty hands touched Sonja's throat.

My sister's skin reddened. She shrieked as if on fire. Her nose bloomed with blood.

My fists trembled, and I almost pounded on the glass, but I feared I could do no good. I was not yet strong enough to save my sister.

And St. Siméon had not saved her either.

I stared with fury and agony at the hideous performance of Uncle Pavan. He no longer held the puppet's strings. Yet its arms and legs stretched forward—one glitter-dusted pink cloth palm reached towards the drops of blood that slid down my sister's face. I held my breath, astounded that the rumors of Uncle's living puppets were true, and I raged inside—as if hot wires twisted within my chest—to see that my sister should be so grotesquely used. I ground my teeth and wished I had knives to throw at the puppet and my unnatural Uncle. To cut them to bits.

Angélique's slender neck twisted as she suddenly turned towards me.

Simultaneously, Gianduja began to swing from his fire-side perch—like a conscious pendulum.

I practically fell in shock. My wonder increased when I saw that while my Uncle Pavan did not touch the strings, one of Angélique's puppet hands shot out without his manual guidance to slap Uncle Pavan's face before he could follow the gaze of his puppets and spot me.

Rushing back from the parapet to the yew tree and clambering down, I sprained my ankle in my haste.

Limping back to my parents, I knew they would rebuke me if I mentioned what I did, so I stayed quiet while horror crawled through my stomach and stabbed my chest every time I thought of my captive sister.

My powerlessness distilled into a self-righteous wrath against my parents. How could they abandon Sonja to our sinister Uncle Pavan and now wrench me away from home? I cursed the city by the sea. I cursed Uncle Pavan. I cursed the morbid appetite of the graceful Angélique. I even cursed God. For not defending Sonja. For betraying me to such a miserable fate.

But I did not curse Gianduja. I pondered his enigmatic gestures by Pavan's fireplace.

In the days ahead, what I had seen at Pavan's blurred into dreams, and the urgency mellowed into a vague unease. I remained disturbed, but belief in Pavan's magic waned. Such things could not really be when the fat old sun still shone.

Father showed me the paper, which included the headline "Master Pavan Takes His Puppets on Parade." The article mentioned some of his talented pupils, giving notable emphasis to Sonja Clermont, "who showed the greatest promise among local puppeteers. Master Pavan has proclaimed that she is 'the best puppeteer of her generation. She comes from a special family.'"

My heart leapt. Not merely from pride and love at seeing my sister praised, but my own opportunity. Uncle Pavan must be thinking of me too. How I also could be a special puppeteer. Even though I loathed him, I could not deny that I still hungered for his validation of my talent.

But then I recalled more vividly the strange horror of what he had been doing with Sonja in the dark of that great old house. I could hardly believe the foul memory. It was still more a bad dream than lucid reality. Perhaps an unseen hand kept a veil in my mind over the raw terror.

"Can't we wait till she comes back from tour?" I asked.

"No," Father said. "We must travel before the next snow comes and buries the roads."

"Will she and Uncle Pavan come visit us in Marseille?"

Father scowled. "It's better if you never see him. He'd be disgusted by what you did with Sebastian. As for Sonja, she will soon be a grown woman. She will go her own way."

I did not understand this talk. Pavan disgusted by my necromantic puppetry? It did not ring true. And surely Sonja would not go her lonely way without her brother or at least visiting her family?

Why do parents lie?

"You will like Marseille," Mother said. "You will enjoy the sea and the many parades."

Why now I wondered? Why when Uncle Pavan had taken Sonja away on tour did my parents relocate us to Marseille? I heard my Mother whisper to Father that "his mind retreats from us . . . as he turns towards his puppets . . ." I strained to hear more but could not.

Father said nothing in reply. But he gently held my Mother's hand, and his eyes flashed at the crackling fire. Of whose mind did Mother speak? Did she mean me? If so, why not use my name and tell me to my face? If she meant the man I hesitated to call "Uncle Pavan" any longer, why point to the obvious? Of course, Pavan would be preoccupied with puppets while on tour. He was a serious artist. But why hadn't he appreciated my talent? Why was I left to stagnate with dull bourgeois parents?

Although the longing to see Sonja fluttered in my chest, jealousy burned from my belly to my throat. At moments like these, my ambition sometimes overcame fear of my monstrous uncle. Broad-winged dreams of greatness eclipsed the pain of separation from my sister. Maybe Marseille, with its reputation as a seaside city of avant-garde art, would appreciate my growing dexterity with rods and strings.

My parents' faces tightened as if expecting some disruptive visitor while they finished packing their boxes. When we pulled up in our coach, I heard them both exhale and their anxious faces slackened as though they now relaxed after a long and intense exertion. Mother spoke again of how I would love to look upon the sea.

Instead of overlooking the sea, we ended up in an apartment above a trash-strewn alley. However, I went on walks with my father to the docks, and we watched fishermen haul up nets of shimmering fish scales and twisted crab claws. Jugglers, fire-eaters, and musicians performed along the piers.

Despite my rage, Marseille's vastness and its many museums and adulation of great artists like Cézanne and Renoir distracted me for a spell. But soon even the presence of the puppet shows at Théâtre Massalia, which I could not afford to attend, and the sublime Basilica Notre-Dame-de-la-Garde, pointing skyward on the hill above the surrounding city, merely reminded me that I lived where my dreams dangled perpetually above me, too far to grasp.

For five years, I burned with fires of frustrated ambition and separation from Sonja.

One day I saw a newspaper headline that emphasized the "sudden collapse" in a show of a "prodigious puppeteer." I read the article carefully. I spotted the name "Sonja Clermont." After touring for months, the strain of an "astounding" performance was blamed for her fainting.

Confronting my parents with the news, I demanded to know how they could remain in Marseille while Sonja suffered.

Father started as if someone had slammed a door behind him. He then took a deep breath and coughed hoarsely as he tuned his violin. Mother, looking paler than usual, glanced from me to Father and stroked at the striated cords of her wrinkled throat.

"Things are complicated," Father rasped, tightening the new strings of his violin.

"How? How can they be so complicated that you don't just bring her home?"

As if jerked by strings, my parents' faces contracted into uneasy lines. They turned their heads away. I pounded my fist on our wobbly stained dining-room table and ran outside. I ran not up to the maze of streets but down the cobblestone avenue toward the sea.

I ran away at last.

II.

Rather than return to Saint Siméon, I stayed for a spell in Marseille. Despite my ambition, I felt a chill run along my neck and dread clench in my chest as I recalled the staring sockets and disconcerting grin of Gianduja and the sinister machinations of Uncle Pavan. I longed to confront him and liberate Sonja, but I was still not ready for that fight.

And so I renamed myself Luc, hoping anonymity and the new name would bring a better life. A chance to gather focus and power till I was ready to challenge Master Pavan himself.

Such opportunity and freedom did not prove truly liberating—just another burden upon my thirteen-year-old neck. Each uneaten meal fed my rage. Each restless night fired my dreams of vengeance.

When begging got me no more than the scraps meant for dogs, I crept down the alley at the first light of dawn, finally persuaded by my aching stomach to sift through the garbage.

I cursed God again as I pulled apart splintery shipping crates heaped high in tilted stacks, hoping for an indication of some discarded but unspoiled grain or only half-moldy potato.

But I found little that might be edible besides acrid rotting cabbage. The vermin of the neighborhood had already stripped clean the fish and chicken bones that clung to or had perforated the rags of cloth sacks that had once held some worthier cargo. Contemplating one purplish-black head of cabbage as though the skull of a hated foe, I ground my teeth in a preparatory gnash of deprived appetite. I tore aside a mud-caked blanket in a last desperate attempt to find something more edible.

Beneath the veil of dirty wool, pressed between a torn leather boot and the comb-like teeth of the gaping lower jaw of a skeletal monkfish, something gleamed in dawn's dusty light.

Stepping closer, the orange glint shone from the eyes of a rumpled face of an androgynous, glass-eyed doll. Its little hand was wedged beneath the boot. I picked up the doll by its limp cloth fingers. It had no other arm, nor did it have legs. Had it once been a puppet?

Children or animals had long ago amputated this refugee. Earwigs fell from its back, but no spiders. I was puzzled by a stamp on its back of "Saint Pierre Asylum" in black letters.

Despite its violent past, there was no open cavity in its belly that might have filled with mold or become the nest of rats. It smelled of earth and vinegar. I hated vinegar. It reminded me of pungent cleansers in the convalescent hospital where my grandmother wheezed her last days to a suffocating death by pneumonia. But vinegar was better than rotten cabbage and fish. And the earthy scent seemed almost fresh to me, a touch of the country here in the crowded city. Something might grow tall and strong from such earth.

I remembered that scent of clean soil from my father's farm, when Sonja and I raced each other while the wind crackled through the stalks and fluffed up our hair as we ran in the corn rows beneath wisps of downy, gliding clouds.

I cleaned the dirty fabric. I polished the eyes and hollowed out the doll's middle. After extracting the stuffing, I stuck in rusted steel welding rods I'd scavenged from a refuse heap, and I inserted my hand. With Mother's sewing kit, I knitted it a new arm and stitched its tears.

No longer a mangled doll, this was now a passable puppet.

I scrounged fishing wire from the sailors at the docks and put on an impromptu show.

I sat on a bench on the pier where the tourists wandered by gawking occasionally at my puppet that sat in front of me on the edge of a bait bucket, waving its arms around while singing a piercing rendition of La Marseillaise.

"Look at the poor little crippled puppet," a girl cooed, pulling at the red ribbons in her hair. "And he's so dirty," she added.

"It's not easy being a crippled soldier, and an artist." My voice rasped from the past hour of high-pitched ventriloquism.

"We're indebted to his patriotic service." Her father dropped a few coins in the bucket.

"What's the little soldier-puppet's name?" The girl took one of her ribbons and tied it around my puppet's stitched arm. "And how did he get that scar?"

"His name is Virgil." I called him Virgil, for I believed he would show me the way out of hell. "He got that scar fighting his enemies. One day he will have his revenge."

The little girl looked at Virgil then back at me. She turned to her father who raised his eyebrows and jerked his head. They left.

I bit into the baguette I bought with my earnings and savored the taste of things to come. I contemplated that once I achieved my inevitable success, I would not miss either tourists or beggars.

Soon, I made more puppets. My performances became lively street theater. Sewing a fishing knife into his balled fist, I made Virgil into a swordsman, who dazzled crowds by the heroic flourishes he used to dispatch the Tarrasque monster of the Rhône.

My skills of puppetry increased daily. Impressed by the digital finesse of my performances, a few friendly thieves showed me I had the dexterity necessary for opening locks. Together, we raided storehouses for finer food to eat and supplies to improve my puppets. I also pilfered new steel rods from a Blacksmith's shop to replace the rusty rods of Virgil.

I bought a black beret, a cloak, and explored more of Marseille. In this disguise it was unlikely I'd be spotted by my parents or the less savory of my acquaintances, whose jealousy of my recent success I was not unaware. However, Virgil and I were not without our defenses.

I located the site of the St. Pierre's Asylum, but the original building had been destroyed, and now a prison stood in its place. There were no answers for me there about the black stamp on Virgil's backside. No matter our scars and brands, we were building our own new lives together.

After a year, I was recognized as the best performer at the waterfront. I no longer had to steal. Local cafés kept me supplied with smoked salmon, croissants, and bouillabaisse from the cast-offs of the fishermen. Soon, I was making enough money to rent my own flat. As I worked on refining Virgil's appearance with fresh paint and cut cloth and rendering his inner mechanisms more responsive with supple strings and wires, it was only a matter of time before I would lose my anonymity as another wandering soul. How long can greatness pass unnoticed?

To be prepared for any unpleasantness that might come with fame, I had purchased puffer fish venom from one of the traders, and I had provided Virgil with a longer and sharper knife.

"Luc, why not join the Carnivaux de Marionettes?" a baker asked. "It's come to town."

"Or move to Saint-Siméon," a one-eared sailor told me, eyeing my bucket of francs.

"That's where Luc's from," Jean-Albert said. "Home of the great Sonja, that prodigy."

Jean-Albert was an older thief—a whore's son from Lyon. He had a puppet of his own, Guignol—Lyon's mascot, who resembled Gianduja. Except he wore a Napoleonic bicorne hat. Jean-Albert had a certain deftness with Guignol. He used his slender warty fingers quite well.

"Where'd this lie come from?" I slipped my right hand into Virgil's handling glove.

"Ah, well, that's going to cost you, Luc." Jean-Albert pointed to my bucket.

I nodded. "Of course." He grinned and took a handful of coins from my bucket.

Then he leaned in close, his breath like rotten peas in my face. "There's a big-bearded man in town with the Carnival of Puppets. He gave a show last night at Château d'If for the prisoners and guards. Talked about how close he felt to Marseille. Said he had a nephew, Elias, a runaway. Someone told him that a young puppeteer worked the docks. This big man perked up like someone had plucked his mighty beard. He put up a reward for you and your blond curls."

Jean-Albert knocked off my black beret, and my wavy golden hair riffled in the breeze.

With a flourish of my right hand, Virgil bared the fishing knife between me and Jean-Albert, who reached for my hair with his long warty fingers.

"You wouldn't be using that little knife on your own friend, would you, Elias Clermont?"

"Perhaps not I, but Virgil has taken a liking to your skin. He may just choose to take it."

"You think your toy can cut me deep enough before I knock your teeth out?"

"Virgil has applied puffer fish venom to that knife, and you will be paralyzed from a single cut. Skinning you will then be a pleasure at our leisure. You and Guignol do as you will."

Jean-Albert released me and stuck his hand in Guignol, who turned his head and seemed to snarl at me and Virgil. "Others might not be so kind with young wharf rats."

I knew it was only a matter of time before I was captured and ransomed to Uncle Pavan.

Unless I improved my disguise. By candlelight while looking into my mirror, I sheared my hair and shaved my head. Rather than dispose of the hairs, I wound them into Virgil's strings. It made me feel yet closer to him.

Having completed my personal transformation, I sold my flat. I also traded my cloak and beret for a monk's robes and hood at a shop that sold both clothes and costumes.

After paying, as I stared at the full-length mirror in the shop, I saw a figure standing behind me in a room full of uniforms and costume paraphernalia. Turning, I saw a giant crow.

Startled, I backed away from this person in a dark robe with a black beak-shaped mask like the plague doctors used to wear in the Middle Ages to keep out the stench of the red death.

"Have you taken your vows?" A breathy voice tinkled from behind the plague mask.

Fearing this was one of Pavan's spies, I ran from the shop and disappeared into alleys.

Before I left Marseille, I saw the parade of puppets that announced the arrival of the Carnival. Behind a pastry vendor's cart, I watched darkly clothed puppeteers slink along with flamboyant puppets which gamboled about to the delight—and sometimes fear—of children.

Near the middle of the parade I saw Pavan—his face painted like a clown—wearing an impossibly large grin that worried me for a moment into believing he had spotted me and was closing in. At his fingertips were perches that controlled not marionettes but attached to other puppeteers, who at a tug and twist from their broad-shouldered master, spun about with their puppets in frenzied dances. Other puppeteers pulled the strings of puppets that controlled yet more puppets, making them tap upon drums or march like an army of a sorcerer's mad minions heading to a siege.

I looked for Sonja but did not see her. I glimpsed Desmond, who had bullied me with his owl puppet. With one gangly hand he made a mouse-puppet scamper before him, and with the other he whirled a flaming phoenix that swooped up its prey to the delight of the cheering crowd.

I cursed him silently for the adoration he received. His insults would not stay unpunished.

I waited until the phalanx of puppets passed. Pavan did not glance towards my hiding spot again, but I could not discern whether he had discovered me or not.

I could remain in Marseille no longer.

I crossed the street and paid fare for a tram to take me inland and into the mountains to the Abbaye Notre-Dame des Neige, that isolated fortress of monks.

Washing dishes and showing how Virgil could bow and cross himself more than earned my keep to secure meals and lodgings with the monks. I continued to keep my hair shorn, remembering my parents' mutterings about some sinister motivation for Uncle Pavan to have stolen my locks. Perhaps my shaved head further endeared me to these quiet industrious men. If they knew what work my walks took me too, out in the dark woods, how together Virgil and I picked our raw materials, they would have marveled at the holy power of my true talents.

My first great discovery was one moonlit night in January with Virgil's damp cloth arms hanging on my neck, as I crunched across the frozen snow into the trees.

A blur of white raced past my feet towards a clump of roots. Beneath this tangle the speedy weasel slipped into its hole. The trailing plume of its flowing tail was not only valuable for its fur. Those delicate yet strong hairs, nearly indistinguishable from the snow, would provide Virgil with subtle sinews, allowing him to do more with his hands than stab with a knife.

I set traps as my father had done to catch the field rats at the farm. Within a week I had caught the weasel. I knocked its head in with a rock. Besides the utility of the weasel's salt-white hairs, the tight skin—once smoked, dried, and treated—would provide a waterproof lining to fit my hand snugly inside Virgil. The tendons, which had directed the weasel's tearing claws, would also serve to make Virgil's legs move when attached to the steel rods with a more fluid motion.

I found the supplies I needed in the monks' workshop. Such nobly self-sufficient men.

Over the course of my fifteenth year, I advanced my work with rods and strings.

Virgil had become a true work of art. I spent the following summer practicing my puppetry in my room and amid the woods surrounding the monastery. I also studied in the library and occasionally performed my puppetry for tourists to earn money. I did very well.

Each franc I earned I counted as a coin of vengeance against Pavan and for the deliverance of Sonja. Yet, I'd be lying if I didn't admit I relished my education with Virgil for its own sake. My favorite hours were in the woods.

I found and trapped more animals to enhance Virgil. I added boar's hooves to his feet and badger claws to the ends of his fingers. Close to my fifteenth birthday in June, I found a dead lynx and extracted its long sharp fangs. I puzzled over how best to construct levers within Virgil to manipulate these new digits and appendages.

It was a riddle I determined to solve before the end of the puppetry festival at Glanum.

Near the close of summer, I had learned of a puppeteering conference to be held on the Fall equinox amid the ancient ruins of the Twin Imperial Temples and sacred spring of Glan.

Although I was young for such a confederation of worthy puppeteers, my application was accepted. Among those stones where once worshippers sacrificed to the Chthonic God and his consorts—a host of puppets danced and glided.

At the puppet conference, the very world of puppeteering was on stage in the colonnaded temples: the fractious slapstick of England's Punch and Judy, the mythic heroism of the elegant kathputli rod puppets of the Rajasthani, the squeaking impressionism of the dabo-dabo puppets Kanuri people of Northeastern Nigeria, and—among my favorites—the sublime storytelling of the intricately painted and punctured Wayang-Kulit shadow figures of Java and Bali.

With great respect, I talked to a Japanese Bunraku master, an omo-zukai, who showed me how the very shape of his fingers had changed over the thirty-year apprenticeship which it takes to do justice to this triple-puppeteer collaboration of one Bunraku puppet. First, the apprentice must take ten years to learn to control the puppet's feet, then another ten years for the left hand, and finally, the master will come to manipulate the head, face, and right hand with a handle with levers in each hand. Even with my talents, I recognized such industry as a daunting commitment to life-eating skill. What satisfaction to count oneself among such masters with their sublimely gnarled hands!

My own destined niche in the world of puppetry had yet to be found. But I knew the gods would not hide their secrets from such a devotee as me forever.

Aside from the range of puppets represented at the festival, it was in the social realm I learned most. More from women than men. One young woman in particular, Fiona Druirmont, captivated my attention. Beyond her pentagram necklace and fairy tattoos, she was, at best, only modestly pretty with short dark hair and rather pasty skin, but her manner and wit were both provoking and enticing.

During the elite seminar of "Virtuoso Techniques of Rods and Strings," not only did I admire Fiona's supple fingers that so deftly pulled strings, but her mind also proved a formidable instrument. I will not deny that my entire being thrilled to hear her talk.

During debates about historical and mythological themes of puppetry, Fiona dispatched her adversaries amid the ancient stones in arguments and ensnared a few visiting professors as her gophers. When during the open-air buffets she proclaimed, "I want chocolate," or demanded, "Where's my coffee?" these distinguished men of learning fetched her whatever she wanted from the catering tents—and quickly.

I saw something new—at least to me—here of the potential for human puppetry.

In the damp cool of evenings, I joined Fiona and other puppeteers, artists, stoners, poets and students in the glades beneath a ceiling of stars.

Soon, Fiona and I entered a world of our own, sleeping in a bag together, speaking of puppets deep into the magical nights. I do not deny that I was falling in love.

Most remarkable were Fiona's rituals of occult puppetry. She was from New York City but had traveled the world, for her parents were diplomats. Also, she traveled widely because of her own work as a translator of French, Russian, and Chinese. She sought out masters of occult puppetry throughout the world. She had learned techniques from a Siberian shaman for earth-divination through which puppets were used to communicate both with spirits of the dead and the genius loci of any place. Farmers still practiced these rituals to ensure healthy crops, and Fiona told me she had seen evidence of such things in the fields between Glanum and Avignon.

I told Fiona of my humble but passionate attempts with the blood of my thumbs and strings to revive my dead pet. I told her what I saw my Uncle do to Sonja one midnight.

She told me that was called "blood alchemy." Pavan was using Sonja's blood to channel the underworld spirits into his puppets.

"You saw the opening steps of the Dance of Blood. A true master of this art can quickly bleed a victim to death or simply rob a few drops to feed a hungry puppet the life it craves."

The horror at this revelation of my uncle's iniquity was only exceeded by my desire to harness that power for my own ends. Finding a dead mouse, Fiona showed me how with a pin prick from her thumb, and metallic fishing line, she could make the mouse twitch in a semblance of life—not merely the work of strings but the spirit that sought out the flesh. Just as Yves had told me on the streets of Saint Siméon. No mere legend, this was a reality. A revelation of magic.

This miracle so moved me that I did not protest when Fiona refused to fully undress in the light. She had an aversion to having her back exposed. Made her too vulnerable. How charming this brave woman would admit such a feeling. I loved her all the more for her honesty.

How I looked forward to necrotic puppetry with Fiona. I had wasted animal carcasses on mere puppet parts—not realizing the spark I could jangle into the cadavers with proper strings.

Fiona told me which festival vendors sold silver and platinum wire, the best conductors to animate the flesh, to bond the elemental forces among essences of human, animal, and spirit. Fiona told me about a man at the conference named Professor Mersault, who had established the Museum of Found Puppetry, which although it had no public building, made use of agents throughout the world to expand the immense and valuable holdings of its collective members. Professor Mersault knew more of blood alchemy than any other. He would be an ally.

I thanked Fiona for all she shared with me. We embraced Virgil between us in the dampness of the night while above our sleeping bag a long-horned beetle gently hummed. For a moment as dawn crept through the spaces between the trees, I thought I felt a pulse start to beat in Virgil's throat, but realized it was just the pressure of my own calloused right thumb.

Each day Fiona and I exchanged more stories of our past, and nourished our dreams for a future where we'd master the art of occult puppetry. Such was our true love.

Her stories fascinated me. I felt the tremor of truth from these revelations of puppetry. How wrong Uncle Pavan had been to make puppets and people his slaves. Puppets are our spiritual partners in this hybrid world of seen and unseen, the living and the dead.

Perhaps Fiona and I would achieve something greater than the world had seen in centuries. A renewal of old ways joined with wild inventions of puppeteering wizardry. Fiona spoke confidently of what might be done together. I felt with her warm fingers in my hand that I could draw the strings of my heart's desire and make the sparks of the stars dance at my command.

The height of excitement reigned that next weekend. We

had competitions between the puppeteers. Beside the Twin Imperial temples, upon a free-standing wooden stage generally reserved for theatrical performances, judges scored the skill and art of our renditions. Although I was not the clear stand-out, I held my own with another nine top competitors, including Fiona. We smiled at each other. I at last dared to believe here was truly a dear friend who would not betray me for gold or power.

Not until the junk puppet competition did I distinguish myself as the king of the festival. Literally grabbing up the refuse dumped from a trashcan, we had five minutes to make a puppet and dazzle the judges. I could keep an ordinary audience spellbound with my hand in a dirty paper bag, but this time I constructed a wonder: A bat-winged serpent with retractable tongue.

The judges clapped. Finally, they would validate the marvels that I could perform.

A dark shape stepped from the woods. A hooded crow. Murmurs spread like a rising wind amid the puppeteers. This was the same stranger with the plague-mask from Marseille.

An elegant Geisha-like marionette dangled from one arm, and from the other hung a frightful, bristle-haired, broken-shell-eyed, pig-demon puppet. That same musical laugh I remembered now jingled amid the ancient stones. Pavan's spy had found me.

The hairs on my neck prickled my skin with a chill but with brave Fiona at my side, I refused to run this time.

Together with my true love, I'd confront this malign stranger. This minion of vile Pavan.

The walk and shape of the person's body confirmed that the minion was a woman.

I glared at her puppets and pointed. "Those aren't junk puppets. Disqualify her!"

Without waiting for the judges to speak, she marched to the stage and her puppets began a mesmerizing dance, better even than Sonja's performances. The thought flashed through my mind that perhaps it could be Sonja herself—but why would she be here and in that disguise?

Such a show followed. I had never seen its equal. The Geisha ran from the demon, but then in a strange contest of wills—emphasized by dialogue spoken in Japanese and Hawaiian—she seduced him. More dramatically, the Geisha revealed through a jerk of the strings that she is a death-figure: her eyes bulged up to brows in cavernous sockets, and her elegant smile erupted in a fang-filled grin. The demon cringed before her. Shockingly wonderful. True virtuosity.

I knew I could make something similar with Virgil. Those boar's hooves, lynx fangs, and badger claws would pop out beautifully once I mastered the art of such trick puppetry.

By some indiscernible fusion of form, these two puppets— Geisha and demon—then combined into a new figure altogether. After juggling five apples, this composite being raised up its four arms to the sky, imploring or demanding a favorable response from the judges.

The judges were silent for a moment, then they clapped with ferocity. I looked at Fiona. Her face drooped, her eyes stared and, as if in a trance, she let go of my hand. We'd been beat.

Despite this performance not being junk puppetry, the best-in-show trophy was offered to the strange crow woman. She spoke not to the judges but to top competitors, including me and Fiona. Her voice came as a murmur. I wanted to hate her, but I admired her grace. Her power.

"If you truly want to learn more of the puppets, come see Le Nez de La Lune. Then go to L'Eclipse in Arles—that is where you will find the most formidable of puppets," said the Crow.

Fiona shook off her torpor. "Who are you?"

The plague-masked spy stepped up to Fiona, grabbed her pentagram necklace and pulled her close.

"Someone who knows blood alchemy far better than a pathetic blood-mule like you."

Fiona staggered back as her nose started to bleed. I never thought I would see her afraid, but she ran away with her face stretched in a pale mask of terror and cowered behind a crumbled pillar.

Despite my concern for hapless Fiona, I did not flinch and held my ground.

Though humiliated at this usurpation of what should have been my hour of triumph—one shared with Fiona—I was impatient to know this peerless puppeteer. If she were not Pavan's agent, might she represent some elite agency of secret puppetry?

Clearly, she knew far more than Fiona did or ever could. This mysterious crow-masked woman stood in front of me, then darted her hand to my covered head. She pulled off my cowl.

"Where is your beautiful hair, now?" Her whisper caressed my ear.

My cheeks reddened. She must indeed be one of Uncle Pavan's spies. And yet, I wanted still to impress her. To show no fear. To prove that I was worthy.

Scorched pride seared my chest just as painfully as when Pavan had only valued my sister's talents and passed me over altogether for the school of puppetry. I had to win over this disdainful prodigy.

She walked away from the puppets she'd left in the middle of the stage and said, "Give my puppets to bald boy. He might learn something. Now stop standing around like you're important." She stalked back into the woods. I gathered up her puppets. Shamed but enthralled.

That night as I rejoined Fiona, she claimed she was too shaken and tired by the day's adventures for amorous pursuits. Despite my reassurances that we were still a prodigious team and fated lovers united in passionate puppetry, she shrunk away from me and my new obsession with the crow-woman.

I grew irritated by Fiona's lack of faith and her galling carnal reluctance.

I peeled off her shirt in the moonlight.

Grinning at me between the sloping angles of her scapula was the inked outline of a mustached clownish figure I recognized too well. His fingers twiddled at the strings of a female marionette with the face of Fiona and the four-legged body of a mule.

Beneath the tattoo were the words, "Fiona, my little fool."

I staggered back. I could barely breathe. I gasped at how Uncle Pavan had defiled me.

Clutching the back of Virgil's spongy head for support, my arms shook at this betrayal.

Fiona pleaded that Pavan had threatened her life. That she truly loved me despite how things seemed. Her eyes, so wide from fear at being found out, enraged me with their craven treachery. I remembered my Mother's words. The venom of a "false heart." How right she was.

Fiona promised not to tell Pavan my location. "I will stay true to you, my dear."

"I agree, my 'dear.' You will never tell him anything. You are truly Pavan's 'little fool.'"

And then I felt the power of inspiration crackle through me.

I seized the strings of Virgil and twirled him in a frenzy. Whether it were the vibrations of the resonant strings or the pulsing anger straining my ears, I heard a hum.

Fiona heard it too, for her eyes widened yet more as she found a new fear. A greater fear.

Something she did not know. Something wonderful that I had come to discover only in that transcendent moment through the mystical gnosis of occult puppetry. A marvel for the ages.

I spun Virgil in a ceaseless whirl. I pulled him into the air.

A gust of wind burst from my dear puppet's mouth. The wind knocked Fiona on her back. Helpless, she could not stop from inhaling the sacred air that Virgil and I had summoned.

Unconscious, she lay shivering in a fever.

I had stumbled upon what I would name the Dance of Disease.

Fiona spent the rest of the conference slowly convalescing from this dire puppet sickness.

If she ever fully recovered, I do not know. After her unmasking as one of Pavan's devious minions, I resolved never to see her again.

III.

I STAYED UP ALL NIGHT WITH VIRGIL. DEPRIVED OF MY SISTER, alienated from my parents, hunted by my uncle, and persecuted by fate so I could not find true love, I focused on improving Virgil. With him, my passion and work were not wasted. With him my trust would not be betrayed.

I cut my flesh between thumb and index finger and inserted the silver and platinum wires, forming hooks which could easily grasp multiple levers in Virgil, even when my fingers were occupied with other machinations within. I thrust my bleeding fingers inside Virgil, who sat peacefully upon the dark ground. As my hands throbbed in pain, I felt the pulse of my own blood but also the ache of bone, the tremor of the earth, the deep quiver of stone.

I would now appear to be a freak to anyone who inspected my hands. So be it. No longer need I hold human hands when through my puppetry I could command the stage of sacred history. I sacrificed family and the dream of love, but my heart must be with my art alone. Not merely the physical craft of performative puppetry, but the epiphanic mysteries that occult puppetry permitted me to penetrate. Into this sanctum sanctorum of wisdom I'd enter with dear Virgil, who was not my creation but my intimate companion in this vale of tears, a partner who helped guide me past each precipice and chasm. He heralded me towards true knowledge, the songs and dances of not only the ancient world but the unseen vistas of a dazzling new horizon. One day, because of our shared purity of desire, we would pull the levers and strings of the cosmos.

In Virgil dwelt something beyond words and memory that had existed long before humanity squatted in dirty huts. I had given him clothes and drawn close to give ear to his voice. I could not take credit for his wisdom and strength. Our union transcended physical puppetry, a spiritual symbiosis beyond religious dogma, deluded mysticism, or bloodless aestheticism.

Whether it were the hum in my head from sleepless misery that spun a vision or the true voice of Virgil that comforted me before blackness came, I knew these words: "Do not despair because of Fiona. She will turn, wither, and die, like the other mortal worms. But I am one of such essence as the deep stones of the earth, and you who have renewed my clothes and enlivened my limbs will share in our everlasting reign over life and death, time and shape." I listened to these words and cherished their truth.

The next day, refreshed despite a short sleep, I brought my newly acquired puppets to Professor Mersault, explaining to him how Fiona had recommended I visit, though she had to leave the conference due to ill health. He welcomed me and appraised the puppets as very rare. He commended me on my deft maneuvers as I imitated the plague-masked woman's performance.

"Those are remarkable puppets," Professor Mersault said. "Each reminds me of the communal theories of divine puppetry. The geisha is at once mortal and empowered by the spirit of death. The demon pig sees with the eyes of the ocean. We eat the pig, and thus we too are infinite. Since Plato in the West, there has been a misapprehension of puppetry as a metaphor for subordination, but earlier forms of animistic puppetry recognized the art as a sacred communion between immortal and mortal, a sharing in the spirit of divine motion. The puppets were more than vessels; they were living bodies of the gods. The puppeteer was a priest demigod, a participant in living divinity."

I enjoyed Professor Mersault's lectures, and he appreciated learning that I was an authentic informant from Saint-Siméon. "Ah, yes, the fool puppet priest, who comes the closest of Western religious figures to the divine communion that characterized primal puppetry of prehistory."

He offered to hire me as an acquisitions agent of the Museum of Found Puppetry.

I accepted his intriguing offer, and we discussed many secrets of occult puppetry. From his books, I learned that the minerals of blood and soil together formed a transcendent energy that galvanized puppetry with an invisible electricity that went beyond space and time.

With the proper materials and the deep bond with the spirits that animate an occult puppet, the adept may cause not only disease and death but madness as well.

Before I left the ancient stones of Glanum, I walked alone

again in the woods. At first, I tried the trick of wire with dead field mice. Like Fiona, I could get them to twitch but not more than that. I was no great necromancer. I was not terribly disappointed since the dance of the living interested me more.

I became consumed with a marvelous idea suggested by Mersault's old books. That one could use a puppet to perform a dance to drive another mad. To twist the thoughts into new forms. To be a magician of mind. Such a subtle art was a nobler skill than force.

To achieve this end, I practiced with Virgil day and night.

I baited squirrels with nuts, and they approached the stump where I sat pulling at Virgil's strings in wild and varied motions. But no matter how inventive I became, the squirrels seemed only interested in the nuts. Traps didn't work, for these were canny squirrels.

I tried next a more direct approach.

I reached out with a nut in my right hand, thrust my finger closer to one squirrel's quivering nose, and the beast bit me. The two incisors crunched through the nail on my thumb.

I swallowed my scream as blood dripped from my thumb down to Virgil's puffy face.

A ripple of laughter came from the woods behind me.

I turned to see the plague-masked crow-woman leaning against a spruce.

Angry at her mockery, the reminder of her humiliatingly astounding performance—and stinging with pain from the vicious squirrel—I ground my teeth and twitched the strings of Virgil.

Rage tensed my arm down to my twisting claws.

Claws that dug into the bark of a nearby larch tree. Yes, a

throbbing pulse of pain connected the rodent and me. Threads of nerve pierced the air, flexed and curled in my hand.

And then I saw the squirrel crawling backwards towards Virgil—whose flat feet, splitting apart like splayed root—had sunk into the ground.

The hands of Virgil dipped and spun in circles, and the smile on his face stretched so tightly above his eyes that it looked as if his cloth head might rip from his fierce grin.

The squirrel turned its head, saw Virgil's antics, and let out a scream that would startle a statue. It ran directly at the tree, rushed up the trunk, along a branch and then jumped off.

Miraculously, the rodent repeated this wild run and leap again and again and again.

Virgil and I called this marvelous creation the Dance of Delirium.

Once the squirrel had fully exhausted itself and stopped moving, I turned around—seeking Pavan's costumed spy.

Pavan's spy had disappeared, back to wherever she went when she wasn't harassing me.

I could now cause both disease and madness.

Soon, I would inflict torment and death.

My job at the Museum of Found Puppetry was a deliverance. Finally, I would have both opportunity and means to pursue my passion for puppets and a fitting revenge. How Uncle Pavan would regret not having picked me as the most apt pupil of my generation.

But stronger than my sense of slight, boiled the rage of righteous disgust. Although I still did not fathom what exactly

Uncle Pavan had done to or with my sister, that vision by his fireplace—in all its hallucinatory and obscene ambiguity—still haunted me during the brainsick hours of the night. Only Virgil kept me from falling into insanity and despair.

When unable to sleep, I would dance with Virgil. Sometimes I thought I could hear him whispering to me of a secret geometry that together we could form to cut through the earth and sky—to open the minds of the old gods to let their very thoughts rush through tunnels of space and time and join us as we whisked about in our subtle paces upon the floor.

We called the choreography of this secret geometric pattern the Dance of the Outside.

As I danced with Virgil in a trance, my thoughts wandered beyond mere revenge to the sublime possibilities of our collaborative efforts. I resolved to prove the marvels of what is possible by pure devotion to the deep knowledge of occult puppetry.

After a year of work handling the records of puppet sales and acquisitions, I had new tools and plans to track down my quarry. These new strategies would free my mind from the protracted persecution of a childhood rent by unbearable loss, a perplexing abduction, and sinister mystery.

Near the end of my second year with the Museum of Found Puppetry, I celebrated my seventeenth birthday with a trip, which Dr. Mersault promised would be most enlightening.

"The gods wait for those who find them. This is one of their secret places." He winked and pointed at the map he'd marked up to help me in the initial legs of my journey.

East of Montignac, beyond where the tourists and anthropologists tend to go, there's a campsite in the hills near

the 12th century village of St-Amand-de-Coly, where vaca-
tioners bathe themselves under the French sun and reflect
how fortunate they are to not live in an age before the auto-
mobile and credit cards. A few miles beyond any trails there
is a small cave beside a sinkhole. The sinkhole itself is reason
enough to bar most public expansion and exploration into
this area, but since it is a matter of public safety, the gap
in the earth appeared on surveyor's maps, and despite signs
warning of the sinkhole, no yellow tape barred the intrepid
sightseer or devoted pilgrim seeking a sacred place of puppet
genesis.

By mid-afternoon I found myself stepping carefully along
the edge of a yawning hole filled with a greenish-brown scum
that served as a watering hole for a couple of wild pigs I roused
upon my approach. After I caught my breath as the swine
ran grunting off into the underbrush, I approached the thick
stump, blasted by lightning and burned charcoal black, which
stood at the bottom of the sinkhole and signaled that the
entrance to the cave was nearby.

I trembled with anticipation as I edged past the murky
pond which the swine had drunk from. I rejoiced that here in
the quiet of woods and sky, I would shortly behold one of the
shrines of primeval puppetry. Who knew what masterworks
of puppet-incantations that it might inspire? What subtle
innovations of rods, strings, blood, and bone?

Sure enough, I saw two shadows in the rocky wall where
the limestone showed ragged and rough as the hill began its
sloping sprawl towards the next ridge. I turned on my flash-
light, stepped closer to the limestone lip, and bent down to
enter the larger of the two passages that constituted the twin
cave openings of Le Nez de la Lune.

Stumbling over the rough tapioca-gray cave floor, I stared at the reddish-brown paintings that were clear to see. Thick-bodied humans, drawn with all the crude clarity of an unusually talented five-year-old with the broad side of a crayon, danced in a ring. In the center of this formation a six-armed two-headed figure both smiled and scowled up at the sky. Stringy yellow lines connected this central figure with the peripheral dancers. I remembered the words of the strange crow-woman from the Glamis festival. What might these pictures mean to her? I wondered if the central figure were some god connected through some threads of nerve or viscera—like an umbilical cord—to its worshippers, and whether the lines suggested simultaneity of consciousness or some as-yet-undeciphered hierarchy of control.

A decade ago, not far from this cave, Professor Mersault himself had discovered mammoth bones with holes containing the dusty DNA of leathery thongs. Professor Mersault speculated that Neandertals staged ghoulish dances of bones that helped conquer the tribe's fear of the elephantine beasts. Perhaps if the children learned to laugh at the big-boned skeletal pliés and pirouettes, they would not hesitate when their spears were all that came between them and the ivory tusks that could pierce skulls and rib-cages in a thunderous thrust that shook the earth.

I imagined staging a parade of thumping bones that would make people today stop and stare at the pale white shambling behemoths of our primitive past, but the inevitable clumsy movements of such lumbering puppets did not move me. I was not convinced either, that the image of this two-headed painting was truly a puppet, but it inspired me nevertheless. The notion of forming something new, something greater than mortal parts, something that raised up its two-heads and stared God baldly in the face, that was something worth attempting. I would make such puppets, and how they would move!

But then as I squeezed Virgil against my chest in joy, I remembered that Virgil was already a great puppet. And together we shared two heads. We were the living incarnation of the art scoured on the rocky walls. Our greatness was because of the unity between our melding minds and the dark and true places of the earth. Whether it were the wind evocatively scraping through the angles of stone or Virgil's actual faint whisper in the cavern's dark, I heard the words, "those who dance in the shadows."

And this roused me to make my own ritual dance of greatness there in the brooding dark.

I waved my hands near delicate helictites sprouting from the walls like frail twisted straws.

I thumped my feet against the ridges of stone on the cave floor.

And with Virgil, I began to circle about, feeling the deep rhythms of the earth.

I knew that we together had begun a mighty new work of truth and terror: the Dance of Stone.

Light-headed from this grand revelation, and perhaps dizzy from the fine dust or faint invisible gas seeping from within the cave, or some mold that clung to the ruffled walls, I withdrew out of Le Nez de La Lune. We exited this time out of the other nostril, thinking there might be something auspicious about completing the loop.

As I emerged blinking in the sunlight, I imagined what other dances Virgil and I could compose in honor of the divine legacy of puppetry we had just communed with. And as the sun flashed on the sinkhole's muddy waters and gilded an aura around Virgil and me outside the mouth of the cave, I envisioned dazzling forms—what marvelous new puppet companions together might we create?

I repeated to myself, "We shall make such puppets. We shall make such puppets!"

A lilting giggle and a splash ended my self-flattering reveries on sublimity.

She stood in the sinkhole's foulness, as though it were her native habitat, from which she had risen. One smooth yellow hipboot's heel planted on the muddy ground while the other boot rose half-hidden in the water as if it were some freshly-bloomed fungus deciding to stir, the crow-beak-masked woman watched me.

Behind that leathery triangular veil, she laughed at me again.

"What do you want?" I grew angry at my fear. Not only anger but curiosity gave me courage, for I knew she must have followed me with purpose. No doubt morbid jealousy obsessed her. She had followed me here to provoke me to some misstep, and then she would reveal to Pavan my failure.

I told her I had grown stronger than she or her Master realized.

She laughed yet again. I looked around at the rocks, the sticks. Perhaps I would give in to my primal rage and throw these brutal objects at her or beat her with them about her head, till all sound stopped, and I could return to the peace of woods and sky.

She spoke in a dry whisper. "You will make such puppets. Such puppets."

— 51 —

"You doubt me? Why do you doubt me? You've seen some of my work."

And then she stood fully out of the water beneath the shade of the twisted flaps of that great stump that squatted at the bottom of the sinkhole.

"I've watched you with your dances of string, your flapping of hands," she said. "But you know nothing until you watch the puppets that dance without string, that rattle without rods, that glide alone on a stage of blood and bone."

I tilted my head and looked down my nose at her. "Do you mean people? Is that your riddle? Or perhaps animals? I have made both dance to my strings. You saw what I just did with the squirrel."

She shook her head and laughed. That light jingle reminded me again of Sonja, and despite my bravado, I shuddered to think what might lurk behind that grotesque mask.

"The dead? Do you mean the dead?" I said. "I have done it. True, only a squirrel so far, but I know I can do it to a person one day! Why do you laugh? Who are you? Reveal yourself!"

She stepped closer, raised lean mud-flecked arms, and partly lifted her beaked mask. Far from hideous were the pale cheeks and liquid white opal of her eye. Was that a grayish tinge to the iris? Whether she were raised in the dark—never having seen the light of sun—or a natural albino, I did not care. At that moment, nothing was more horrible to me than that flaky white skin and those translucent milky eyes.

I recognized some features—chin, cheekbones, hair—of my sister Sonja, but I couldn't bear to look at her directly for more than a second.

If I screamed, it must have been the inevitable reflex of simple shock. Yes, I ran away.

She shouted after me, as my running feet crunched on brittle fragments in the forest of dead and dying trees.

"Mother and Father have gone home, Elias. I will see you in Arles, beneath the arena."

When she said my name, I almost stopped and ran to her. A pang trembled through me.

My dear sister, my only friend in the world. Her soft, wise, gray eyes bleached by dark puppetry to ivory. The aching long in my chest made me gasp, but I kept running.

I couldn't turn back. I remembered Fiona had nearly ensnared my heart and delivered me to Pavan. I dared not walk straight into another trap. I wasn't yet ready to confront him.

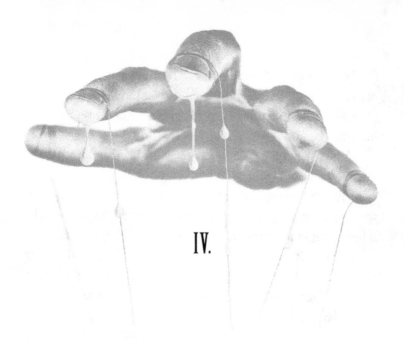

IV.

WHAT DID IT MEAN THAT SONJA HAUNTED MY STEPS? HAD
Pavan made her into a mere minion, such as Fiona? Could
I never again trust my flesh-and-blood? My family had proven
too weak to sustain the greatness that was within me. And
yet, the thought of my parents having returned to our old
home burdened my chest with additional pressure, an anxiety
to see them once again. It was one of many reasons that before
the trial that would await me in Arles, I wanted to revisit
Saint-Siméon. Even if Sonja had lied to me. Even if she were
Uncle Pavan's creature.

I sent notice to Dr. Mersault that I would take the rest of
the summer for vacation.

I traveled in secret and only at night. It took me nearly a
month to return home. In the dark nights as my feet clomped
on dirt and stone, Virgil and I created new steps in the
dance born from our wanderings across and below the earth.
Inspired by our revelation of the cave, how we longed to

perfect and perform this mighty Dance of Stone when we got to Arles.

Together we would usher in a profound aeon, perfecting the bond of mutual gnosis between man and puppet.

If at Arles we were not received as heroes and icons of the elite potential of occult puppetry, then the audience surely must be unworthy philistines. We then would judge them.

On the streets of Saint Siméon, I walked incognito. After keeping an eye out for Pavan's spies, as well as my old friend Yves—and seeing none of them—I decided to try my hand with my puppets. Rather than reveal Virgil to one of Pavan's spies, I decided to use one of my recent creations—Penelope, Virgil's courtesan, whom I set next to a dollhouse in the town square, a permanent stage for puppeteers.

Penelope's performance won a few claps. But for a town that had seen the virtuosity of Sonja and had its own school of advanced puppetry, I am afraid I did not awe them. As Penelope danced up and down the stairs of the dollhouse, the crowd eventually got bored and left. Even if their dogs regarded me warily—and one of them threw its head back and howled at the site of my uncannily adroit skills—the people themselves did not fully recognize my prodigious art.

Despite the delicacy with which I directed Penelope's every step, and the passion with which I strained her face into a grimace of grief, the spectators decided they had seen the best of my tricks. They wandered away to their gambling establishments, opium dens, and whorehouses. Or simply to a family dinner where roast mutton waited for rending, digestion, and excretion. Perhaps their hounds puzzled over what they had seen as they gnawed the mutton bone marrow.

I had at least garnished some francs from the more courteous spectators. I had my scraps.

Unfortunately, my money had attracted the attention of a beggar, ruined by opium, dancing on the strings of his perpetual addiction. At least in my most desperate times, I had not started down the perilous path of those who sold their souls to the bulbous poppy blooms.

He tugged at my coat. His palsied hands shook with his need. "Donne-moi d'argent."

I told him I had no money to give him. He raised his hands, and I smelled then the rank stench of garbage. Fish guts. Moldy potatoes. He had been in the alleys going after what he could. My stomach lurched as I remembered my time in Marseille. I looked at him directly and saw the sallow jaundice in his eyes.

For a moment, I pitied him. But his tone quickly alienated me.

"Oh, you don't have nothing to give, eh? But you would give plenty for that Yves, wouldn't you? That failed puppeteer!" He pulled off my hood before I could shove him away.

Staggering back, he laughed and pointed. "I know you, bald or not—Pavan's ward. Charity case that couldn't even make it into his school. Your family was not much, were they? Only your sister had value. Well, at least her eyes certainly fetched a price."

Despite my repulsion and outrage at this vile messenger, anxious longing leapt in my chest. "What do you mean? Here's money enough for you." I pressed coins into his stinking palms.

"Oh, haven't you heard? After fainting at too many shows, she also went blind."

At my look of shock, the beggar laughed again. Then he continued his tale. "She had to sell her eyes for money for the puppets they use in Arles. I sometimes do that dirty work myself. My last job was procuring the kidneys of your failed street puppeteer, Yves. Like that poor inept fool, the children who don't make it as puppeteers, their organs are worth something even if their fingers aren't. Isn't it wonderful that a star like Sonja can fall off her high and mighty stage but still have something to offer to the world of puppetry?"

My words rasped from a dry throat. "You're lying. I saw her a month ago. She was fine."

"Ha, it was but a fortnight when she went blind. Her eyes blanched like a sick oyster's pearls. You've come too late. Pavan sends his sorrowful condolences, oh misguided Elias."

I do not know what exactly seized me then. If it were primarily my fear and horror about Sonja's fate. Or my passionate rage at the insolent beggar's abominable words—even though I couldn't quite believe them. Or maybe it was a colder contemplation of this detritus of humanity being fit for a suitable experiment that goaded me into the next step I took. Pity drained out of the bottom of my soul.

Perhaps somewhere in the murky pool of my self-awareness, hearing the name of my uncle combined with this new hateful tale about my sister brought back the vision of my uncle's midnight performance with my terrified sister.

Something powerful—whether memory or vengeful rage—inspired me to jerk Virgil's strings so that he jigged the Dance of Blood—the ancient form that Pavan had used to sap my sister's strength to raise the spirits of the earth into the arid cloth of his misbegotten puppets.

As I watched the beggar cringe before the wild gesticulations of my prize marionette, a new kind of lust rose in my belly for something more than what I had done to Desmond or squirrels.

Perhaps I'd do the Dance of Delirium.

How delicious it would be to see the man be driven to something extraordinary: would he make like a maddened squirrel and scale the clock tower and leap into the air? At the very least, he might bash his face into a bloody pancake on the pavement or tear out his hairs in wild abandon as Virgil's arms curled into twirling vines that dug with crisp slivers of green and yellow into the thick gray cobblestones of the town square.

But the Dance of Blood proved enough.

The man grew redder in the face until a single drop of blood ran down from his left eye.

"Stop," he squealed like a leaky water pipe. "I can tell you more about Arles."

I ended the dance, listened to all that he could say beyond his previous vile boasts.

"At Arles," the beggar gasped, "there is a ritual, and if Pavan finds favor through it, he will be crowned Archon of all the puppeteers."

Pavan's foul stooge could give little in way of further detail, so I turned away, not needing to see the blood run from his nose, ears, and mouth as he moaned and rolled about on the street. His sacrifice to the Dance of Blood, which Virgil and I had perfected, did not mitigate the offense I took at the contemplation of Pavan receiving a superlative honor he did not deserve.

Walking past my parent's farmhouse I stopped myself from approaching the door. I could see my father playing the violin near the window as he looked off into some distant memory. Mother sat at the table, knitting yet another sweater of protection against the evil eye. How homely and disappointing were my parents. By what strange ministry had they been led back here? Could they not even hold to their decision to move and live in Marseille? What dance of cowardice and regret played at their bourgeois strings? And yet I had to bite my lip and jerk my head away lest I shed a tear, knock at the door, and beg to embrace them.

Before leaving town, I revisited Pavan's mansion.

Climbing the same yew tree of my boyhood, I surveyed the property. The premises was dark. Pavan must have already departed for the great festival of occult puppetry in Arles.

My time at the docks had well-equipped me with the necessary skills. Luck also favored my enterprise. No servants or angry dogs rushed to intercept me as I approached the kitchen window, pried upon the hinge, removed the pane, and entered.

For the basement door I used my screwdriver to dismantle the lock, which was barely a challenge. Lighting the lamp with a match, I saw I stood on no floor but hardened mud. Suspended on several rows of wires hung what at first glance appeared to be clusters of leafy heads-of-garlic. As I drew closer, I saw these were puppet heads whose hair looked to be a mixture of flax, silk, wool, and human sources.

There were names above these heads, at least half of Saint-Siméon represented by humanoid figures of cloth, rod, and string. I thought I recognized the mayor of Marseille as well, his curly hair tangled with clumps of moss. The feet of the puppets were hidden in pots sunk into the dirt floor. I thought of what Professor Mersault had said of the spirits of the earth, and I trembled—not with fear—but excitement at the revelations and power soon to be claimed.

I drew Virgil from my backpack. With hands pulsing with the determined beat of my heart, I edged him closer to inspect this storehouse of homunculi puppets. Already, the soil quivered in the pots as we stepped about, looking to find the effigies of my family.

And there they were: Patrick Clermont and Anne Belleau. Yellow-tails of nightshade flowers hung from their creviced mouths like perverse pacifiers. I understood this form of sympathetic magic. This was the sinister method by which my parents—Father, antlers stuck on either side of his cushiony head, and Mother with red lipstick—were kept silent by Pavan.

Beside these forms were two empty spaces with labeled names, "Elias" and "Sonja."

I dug out the poisonous plants from the mouths of my parents' doppelgänger puppets. The puppets croaked drily in the damp of the basement. Holding Virgil and my ears close to their mouthing flaps, I could distinguish only one word, "Arles."

I removed the antlers from Father's head, sewing them carefully into Virgil's thick scalp. Why waste? Virgil was now King of the Forest, a proud Horned God, and I smiled at the irony of cuckoldry and royalty that Pavan might fail to appreciate. An electric thrill of anticipation ran from Virgil up my arm. His grip tightened against the string, pulling me towards the door.

But I was not ready to leave town. I searched for the name "Desmond," but did not find it. Why not? Perhaps Uncle

Pavan kept certain effigies with him for more immediate control?

Although I knew it to be unwise, I visited the school before heading to Arles. The dormitories on the edge of the marble-and-brick building housed assistants to the instructors as well as the students. I had no doubt that oh-so-dexterous Desmond had earned the rank of one of these pedagogical assistants. Near the dormitory entrance on a bronze plaque listing residents, I found his name and address.

At the edge of his first-floor window—open no doubt to enjoy the fresh breath of a July night—I saw Desmond's downstairs quarters were unoccupied.

I stepped through the open window with Virgil.

Climbing the stairs, I enjoyed the feel of my skin stretching and contracting as I flexed Virgil's claws and bared his lynx teeth, oily with the crystalline sheen of the puffer fish elixir.

An owl fluttered towards my face, and I heard it call my name. A fist struck my nose.

"Pavan warned me you might come visit. You and your petty jealousy. Pathetic nobody!"

Desmond had heard me enter his residence. He laughed as he struck me again in the head. He'd grown taller since I'd seen him. A man with shaggy sideburns and long arms. He hit just as hard as I thought he might. Harder even. My head ached from the impact, and I grew dizzy.

Desmond's hands proved as fast as his fists were hard. While I wobbled from the blow, his owl puppet bit my earlobe, and the blood trickled down my neck.

"And what is that? Pure absurdity!" Desmond pointed at Virgil's horns.

And then came a flash and a boom. The showy phoenix puppet rose from the floor in a wreath of flame. The top of my head already burned, I shielded my eyes with my left hand.

A dramatic little show.

Now it was our turn. Virgil clambered up those long legs of Desmond, digging in cloven hooves and slicing claws. Desmond screamed as Virgil butted him in the stomach, sharp horns perforating soft flesh.

And then Virgil bit him on the shoulder with those Lynx fangs glazed with puffer fish venom. It wasn't long before Desmond sunk to the floor, his lips numbing, and his hands quivering uncontrollably. He could not even raise his head when I cuffed his ears.

"Mercy. Please. Mercy."

"Nobody is here to give you mercy."

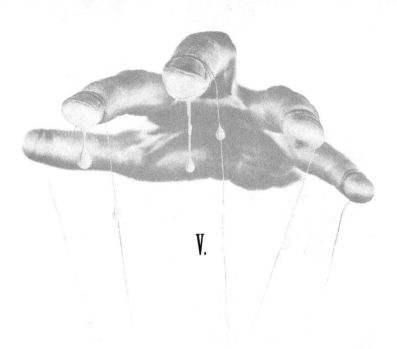

V.

I SPENT A LONG NIGHT REHEARSING DANCES WITH VIRGIL. WE bled Desmond gradually until sure he'd told us all he knew of Uncle Pavan and Sonja. Yes, she was blind, but he had no idea what exactly Pavan had done with her. Pavan had told Desmond that "he would know what secrets he should know when he was ready to know them." Desmond was a mere lieutenant. Pavan was the emperor. And what of Yves? Desmond never paid him attention. His body "more useful dead than alive." When I asked Desmond to tell me more of what occult puppetry Master Pavan knew, it was as though something jerked back his tongue. He would say no more. I nodded to Virgil.

And then Virgil began with mincing steps the Dance of Delirium.

I left Desmond, paralyzed and staring at stars he had never seen, flashing from a distant sky.

Not far from Arles, I parked my rusty bike near a farmer's field because I had spotted a peculiar sight. It was no ordinary scarecrow that I saw but some preparatory stage of a puppet. A ring of dead crows lay in the wheat around the effigy, and as I drew closer I saw that sitting in the sockets of the gourd-like head on a stick were human eyes. Were those Sonja's eyes? They looked grayish like hers, but I hoped I was merely preoccupied with the ravings of that beggar.

A brown, pinkish clump stuck out of the folds of the waistcoat binding the figure's belly. Poking at the stomach with a stick, I saw two kidneys scrunched inside the stuffing. Were these once poor Yves's? I left this foul scarecrow and considered what other crude horrors this meant I might face in Arles. If intended to frighten me away from puppetry, these depraved fools would find I had terror to share as well.

It was almost sunset when I traveled the wooded path through the fields, which would take me onward to Arles. I admired the orangish light filtering through the gray-white branches of the spreading plane trees that flanked the canal. Then, I spotted the crossroads ahead where must sit the sign of the shortcut to Arles the beggar had mentioned. Soon I would be in town.

Above the sign, someone had capriciously hung another scarecrow, limbs connected by rope to several trees to suspend the figure as though hovering in a web. At first I was tempted to play at this found marionette to practice and enjoy my craft, but then I saw the pale flesh of thin arms, the silver flax of Sonja's hair.

There was no denying that this was Sonja, my dear sister. But did she live?

I quickly inspected the arrangement of ropes. I estimated I could free her without breaking her neck from the resulting torque or fall. I drew out one of my leather-cutting knives. Untying and cutting the knot of the central rope round the nearest plane tree, I lowered her slowly. She landed limply in the dirt. I sprang forward and cut the remaining ropes from her wrists, ankles, and waist. She turned her face towards me, and I saw ulcerating wounds in her throat and belly that I could not hope to heal.

She had no eyes, and she bled heavily, but it was still Sonja.

White hot rage stiffened my resolve not to break down in front of her, but to avenge this sacrilege. This outrage against my family. My love. My art. Misery boiled my vitals.

Beware Pavan, I will make you pay.

"It's me," I said. "It's Elias."

"I heard what you did with Sebastian"—the first words from her blood-clotted mouth.

"I was a child, Sonja." And I took her hand at last.

She spoke as though her words were a thick porridge that she had to disgorge. "Your instinct was right. When Pavan learned of your talent from a neighbor, he sought you out, but you were gone. He recovered Gianduja. Tried to bend you to his will, but you have always been too strong. I wanted to tell you before so many times, but Pavan had a hold on my tongue and blood. He's let go now. He took what he wanted." She hiccupped. Blood leaked from her lips.

Though I begged her not to talk, Sonja whispered fiercely through convulsions of blood the story of our family—secrets unspoken for too long on lips sealed by Pavan's tug of occult strings. Father was not only a French violinist of high caliber but a Freemason and an inventor. He'd been renowned for miraculous constructions of wire and metal.

A wealthy man, Pavan, endowed Father with great riches to help him work, but in truth Pavan only sought to steal Father's techniques. Mother, a Gypsy dancer, who gained attentions not only from Father but his dangerous benefactor, Pavan. Pavan's true contract was not with Father but with malign spirits of forbidden alchemy, whose sinister strategies he combined with Father's brilliant methods of conductive metallurgy. Father became indebted to Pavan.

Sonia explained that Pavan was no uncle to either of us, but a monstrous father to her. A mysterious man of many names, a successful inventor himself, and his money had bought him men and women who served him literally until their deaths. He specialized in occult experiments that tested human capacity for suffering and validated necromantic theories of blood alchemy.

Our mother had no choice. Pavan's powers of compulsion were too much.

Pavan acquired Father's fortune, impregnated Mother to birth Sonja and then commanded our parents to raise her close to the soil so that spirits of the grasping earth would be near. At school, Pavan was many pupils' "uncle" but no woman's husband.

Pavan hoped through his thaumaturgic experiments to soon be everyone's immortal god. He had stated his belief that he would be the Archon of the great will that animated not only occult puppets but all things of light and darkness.

"Enough about Pavan's despicable conceit. And what of me?" I asked Sonja. "Were my parents what they seemed or were they minions of Pavan?"

"They were yours. They were true." I knew Sonja meant to soothe me with this answer. She did not understand that I would rather have heard that some invisible spirit had crept past both my "parents" and Pavan. I wished such a being had raised me up from some underworld to sprout here, an unequalled avatar among tiresome mortals. I despised my mortal roots. Why settle for the mundane when the sublime beckoned?

As my mind spun, I was glad I had Virgil to comfort me. If I had not trusted in my bond with Virgil, I might have beaten my fists together in rage at this revelation of a hum-drum birth. Yet, as I considered my fate, I consoled myself with the realization that my triumph should be all the greater because of the scale of my Olympian ascendancy from such humble seeds.

Virgil and I scoffed at Pavan's despicable pretensions at divinity. Yes, an enterprising man, but a foolish upstart in the greater hierarchy which Virgil and I were destined to enter. Together as the rightful and worthy adepts of the true art, Virgil and I would make Pavan pay for his loathsome hubris.

We listened with furious wrath as Sonja explained how Pavan had shown her the forbidden dances so young that all happiness faded from her soul. He had farmed, harvested, and bled Sonja as a vessel to chthonic powers. He'd fed her the illusion of a nuclear family to fuel his own powers of occult puppetry. Her eyes had seen things which drained her very being of vitality.

After a fit of coughing, Sonja said, "he would have used you next." Through her wheezing speech she explained how only her hunger of vengeance remained while Pavan bent her to his will. But there was no hope to give her vengeance wings until the night when I had come to Pavan's home. She had glimpsed me at the window, though she'd given no sign when I witnessed how Pavan paraded Angélique in her dance of blood. The coy puppet had turned its head to look at me, but it had stopped Pavan with a slap before he too could see me staring. Gianduja, that treacherous rag, had tried to betray me. But Angélique's slap came from a great will beyond both Gianduja and Pavan. Sonja knew it was a source from which she too might draw. Pavan himself was but a puppet before that great will.

I recognized the truth of her words. I had misjudged Angélique and falsely trusted Gianduja. But now I was becoming in harmony with that mighty will beyond. A force that spun in the infinite dark long before men mumbled in their caves about gods and fate, death and souls.

Despite her growing powers of blood alchemy and her communion with the deeper pulses of earth, bone, string, and rod, Pavan and his men had used parasitic spells upon her and strung her up here to die exposed to the cold night, for they feared treachery and wanted to siphon off her powers while they were so ripe. Before she had sold her eyes for francs to the mysterious puppeteers from Arles, she had stolen for me a page from Pavan's books. She pulled a handful of francs from her pocket and gasped her final words. Before a final slump of her shoulders, she made me swear that I would "avenge Pavan's defilements. Whatever the cost."

A page in her back pocket contained the excerpt, "Of Golems, Humunculi, and Puppets."

> Although the holy or infernal names serve
> for activation of golems, it is only blood
> and electricity which will galvanize the
> bodies of the homunculus and the puppet.
> It is recommended that the adept solely use
> blood for which he can vouch for its purity,
> preferably the fresh fluid of a family member—
> ideally one's own progeny. Convention frowns
> upon incestual practices, but the animal spirits
> may best be harnessed when consummation has
> cemented bonds of love and duty to paternal
> authority. He who would be Archon of the
> Supreme Will must not be fastidious or timid.

I pocketed the money she'd given me. In a daze I stroked the ends of the thin hairs on my sister's arms, brushed aside her matted hair and saw on the top of her neck the scabbed tattoo of a clown mustached like Pavan. From each large hand dangled skeletal puppets, one with the initial "S" and one with the initial "E." I thought of Fiona, but I knew well the difference between false lover and dear sister.

Despite the sinister threat suggested by this tattooed picture and the sheer outrageousness of what Pavan's magical book indicated was required to achieve supremacy in occult puppetry, I chose not to resist the impulse to enter into intimate understanding with my dying sister. I knew I had no authority of any kind over my sister, other than the burden of imperative vengeance. At first I could barely breathe as I considered Sonja's words—"whatever the cost". I knew she had anticipated in her wisdom exactly this eventuality. My mind grasped what was inevitably required, but my cowardly flesh would not cooperate at first.

Behind my ear, in my backpack, I could hear Virgil urgently whispering in his scratchy voice about what I must do. I must not be "fastidious or timid" when such power beckons. Virgil guided me to do that which I alone could not have had the strength. I felt then how Virgil completed me and my sister. Together we had formed a triumvirate that destiny had summoned to wreak justice upon a fallen world. To the unitiated we were the vilest of sinners, but in the glory of what we would achieve, we were the most courageous and enlightened puppets dancing in wondrous communion with the Supreme Will unseen behind the stars."

With clenched jaw and set eyes, I retied my sister's body and hung it back up in the trees.

No one passing in the shamed hours of the night could have understood the delicate mystery that bonded us together in flesh. The subtle ministry of digit and string. How that ultimately loving spirit of communal motion bound us as one being. How her tendons and ligaments jiggled beneath the creaking branches in the quiet dark.

After I was done, she was indeed dead.

No breath or pulse remained. But the Supreme Will that joined us endured.

I feared the bards would sing unfairly of the deed with Virgil, me, and my sister, but they should also sing of the ferocity with which Virgil and I would dispatch Pavan, whose evil had made the shame necessary.

And now, my cheeks wet with tears, my hands red with

blood, I would get to Arles with Virgil at his full strength beside me.

Pavan would know terror, most pure and sublime.

Virgil and I stood in silent sympathy, ready to perform our tour-de-force, the Dance of Stone.

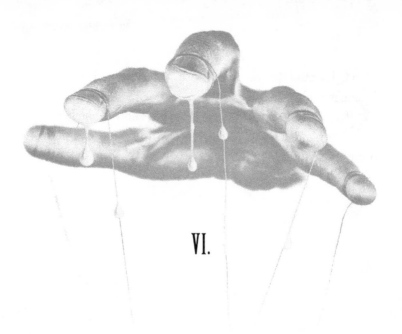

VI.

MOST PEOPLE ASSOCIATE BULLFIGHTING WITH SPAIN, BUT France too maintains its traditions of sparring with the pointed earthly incarnations of the Horned God. No one but those in esoteric orders of puppetry, however, have learned of Arle's Eclipse, the festival of occult puppetry that coincides with those days witnessing the total eclipse of the sun. I had come to the right place.

Down the stairs, presumably for maintenance workers, there was a room, empty except for some wooden cartons, and a revolving door. On its face was a type of chromatrope, a glass device whose rotation produces moving lights upon a screen—a tool for the projection of shadow puppetry. This one had some sort of outline of two figures, one blue and one red. There was no screen in the room, so I surmised it must await on the other side of the door.

As I passed through the door, I entered a much larger and darker candlelit room where stood a silky white screen, along which blue and red twisting figures embraced in either a frenzied dance of love or a desperate struggle of hatred—I could not tell which.

A thin man wearing a fool's cap and grinning as he watched me sat at a desk near this screen, and he motioned me over. His skin looked so white I wondered if he spent his days and nights underground, perpetually serving as doorman to ongoing gatherings of occult puppeteers.

"Care to wager tonight?" he asked.

"Perhaps, but I'd also like to compete."

"Oh?" He grinned again and leaned forward with a pin to prick at my wrist.

I drew back.

"Don't worry," he said. "It's sterilized."

"But why the blood?"

"Why?" Yellow eyes narrowed at me, and the bells jingled as he leaned back in his chair. His face smelt of coconut oil and his pale waxy complexion seemed almost a façade in the candlelight.

"Because they like to get a taste of you who are going to touch them," he said.

"Who?"

"The puppets of course." He frowned. "Don't get something for nothing in this world. The puppets choose their handlers here. Haven't you heard we still practice the Old Art?"

"I have come for precisely that reason. My chief puppet knows the Old Art. We've chosen each other and have become quite proficient together already."

"Have you? Well, I'm sure that won't amount to much here since you and your puppet are both newcomers, but you are bold for trying your skill with the masters within. And may I inquire who told you about the Eclipse?"

"My uncle," I said. "Pavan."

"Ah, your uncle. Remarkable." The jester stared for a moment as though I were a hapless ghost. "Now that's a puppeteer, Pavan. He's already here, of course. But you're rather late, eh? Best be going in. You wouldn't want to miss the trials. Now, just a few drops."

I let the man prick my hand with the pin, which was no worse after all than a quick sting.

"And the one-hundred francs." He opened his pale hand and waited for my payment.

Thanks to Sonja's gift of francs and yet more in my pockets from my work for Professor Mersault, I readily paid the unexpectedly high fee and walked past the screen.

Though snug in my pack, Virgil's laughter rattled in my ear. I smiled in sympathy. We were far from "newcomers" to the Old Art.

The room beyond had no clear borders. I could not trace its outlines in the dim light of the candle chandelier that hung from the ceiling.

As I walked deeper into this underground chamber, an immense painting blocked my path, an old rendering of Hell's Mouth. Lanterns in front of the painting illuminated red-faced demons chortling and cavorting as part of some absurd war in heaven.

At the center of the painting opened a tunnel, dripping with sounds of water running into a drain. One had to advance through the painting.

A humid breeze caressed my face as I walked into the tunnel, and I heard murmurs of people talking. An occasional curse. And then a high shriek, which ended abruptly. A pause in the murmuring—then all repeated much the same. Voices like parrots imitating men, the barks of dogs, the buzzing of a late-night at a bar, clicking and humming—the puppeteers were at their business. Their hubbub reminded me of my childhood dreams when I played violin on a stage before an unearthly audience. Finally, another chandelier was visible. And beyond it a huge chromatrope, grander than the one at the entrance. It swirled with dazzling colors.

In the cavern beyond I saw tents where merchants from all over the world sold a variety of exotic wares. I saw a platform where a group had gathered. And I saw—even more prominently—that near the platform was a pit, behind which on the edge of the gloom, appeared to be yet another screen.

This screen was huge and reddish, and the outlined shapes of puppets showing beyond it were also much larger than any I'd ever seen. They loomed most strikingly, these stark shadows on that scarlet cloth. I scented the sweet smoke of coconut oil which must have lit the lamps of the chromatrope. The yellow, white, violet, and green lights of the chromatrope somehow did not dilute those shadows.

I marveled at their prowess, these deft practitioners of shadow puppetry upon that more distant screen. Surely not even their Javanese antecedents demonstrated greater skill than these wielders of rods and string. The sheer subtlety!

Such supple fluidity that emanated from flapping silhouettes. Some of the twisting movements astonished me—one wormlike thing wavered with several rows of eyes and what looked like long tusks. This puppet rose and dipped with such delicate undulations of its serrated abdomen, expanding and contracting like a spiraling accordion. I was dumbfounded how such detailed differentiation of form and movement could even be possible.

Nor did it seem viable how this puppet was able to rotate in such a fashion that no puppeteer became visible behind the scarlet screen. No doubt the handlers were crouched low, and the refraction of the light hid their stealthy gestures. Or perhaps like Balinese puppeteers, they hid themselves in the folds of hanging fabric akin to the giant Barong Landung puppets. I was in the presence of the epitome of greatness. The apex of puppeteers.

With such prodigious skill showcased, we had to be at our best. Inside my backpack I felt Virgil tremble, alert and eager to emerge to reveal what greatness we had achieved. Could Pavan or another competitor beat us by some underhanded trick? Yes, and the full extent of these other puppeteers' powers was still not known to us, but with Virgil I knew we were unlikely to be caught off guard.

I longed to peer behind that scarlet veil to behold the shadow masters of such vital illusions. I removed Virgil from my pack and shared the sight with him.

As Virgil's noble horned head poked up in the dappled darkness of the cavern, my right hand either acted in accord with a hesitant and alien hemisphere of my brain, or it was Virgil himself who independently pointed with one of his padded and clawed hands towards the platform. Whether the movement of Virgil's hand would have been registered as either obeisance or defiance by the onlookers, I do not know since they gave no response. Above the platform, numerous puppeteers clad in crimson, gold, and silver robes sat on a dais. Their stone thrones were carved from the walls of the earth. These gaudy puppeteers watched a tall red-coated man approach a puppet that stood yet taller than him.

As I drew closer to inspect the crowd, leaving for now the wondrous shadow puppets working their magic on that scarlet screen, I realized that the puppet towering above the tall—and bald—man on the platform was the very puppet I had seen in the field, masquerading as a scarecrow.

It stared with the borrowed eyes of some unfortunate stranger—no, surely those were Sonja's gray eyes! No longer pale as bleached coral but her own gray eyes looking directly at the man who approached waving his large hands—not unlike a man nervously offering something tempting to pacify or distract a dangerous animal.

This tall man on the platform I recognized as my Uncle Pavan. Was he undergoing one of the trials the doorman had alluded to? The scarecrow puppet's vigilant posture suggested it might be some sort of a sentinel or even a gladiator.

Pavan had a smirk despite his tentative gestures, and he abruptly tugged at the left side of his thick mustache.

He seemed to be signaling to the men and women on their stone thrones in the dais above the platform. They silently watched this standoff between man and puppet.

Behind the platform on the cavern walls hung immense bones. No doubt mammoth limbs from bygone days. Perhaps even sacred tools of puppetry of which Professor Mersault had taught me about at the Museum of Found Puppetry, and I had seen with my own eyes in the cave art at Le Nez de La Lune.

This nexus of mysterious puppet, mutilated sister, and arrogant enemy troubled me. Although I hated Pavan, I could not help but feel an involuntary concern for my false uncle. Perhaps it was merely the sympathy of understanding the professional pressure—for he seemed about to perform some act of great technical difficulty against a formidable adversary and before a demanding crowd.

I pitied him, yes, but I also wished to watch him fail. I sensed great power from that puppet with my sister's eyes. He would have no easy time with it.

"Pavan!" I yelled. "You are no match for this trial. Stop before you are destroyed. You are not fit to be Archon. That is an honor that shall belong to me alone."

The scarecrow puppet stood still as if listening. And those gray eyes of my late and dear sister regarded me with a coolness that sent prickling chills down my neck.

Pavan glanced towards me as if he didn't know who I was. He returned his gaze to his puppet adversary and took a step back. A yellow light from the chromatrope caught his face, and in that golden reflection his eyes appeared watery and sickly—much like that jaundiced beggar.

"Your usual tricks will not help you here, Pavan." He looked again towards my voice.

Pavan saw me clearly at last. His eyes creased and widened as he also noticed Virgil and his antlers.

"I do not need your counsel, you miserable dilettante. I see by your theft of my artifacts you have adopted the criminality of the company you kept in Marseille. Perhaps young Clermont, you might have been great. But you are nothing but a thief and a coward and a detestable amateur!"

I caressed the antlers upon Virgil's head. "I have stolen nothing, but liberated my parents' souls from your keeping. You had best look to your own soul next, for prophecy is upon me, and I have the courage to speak it. The puppet you face there is nothing less than a revenant of my sister's wrath, which will destroy you. Give up your strings and rods and leave this place in the disgrace you deserve. For I may be an amateur, but I am your better by far, and should you dare to face me, I will beat you soundly."

Pavan glanced again at the gray-eyed puppet then curled his lip and spat on the wooden floor of the platform. His booming voice reverberated through the cavern. "It is you, Elias Clermont, son of a cuckold and a whore, who will be beaten here. You are no match for me. I am undaunted by your 'prophecy,' young fool, and I am even less impressed with your puppetry, upstart. You never were as talented as your sister."

"More of your filthy lies and pathetic boasts, Pavan." My voice grew shrill with the lust of expectation and vengeance. I cannot deny his words hurt me, but I knew that with stung pride I would savor my revenge all the more.

While Sonja's strange puppet doppelgänger stood by, the group of puppeteers and their inhuman companions all watched us and listened intently to my righteous charges against Pavan, who waved away my words as if swatting gnats.

I thrilled to my moment of truth and indulged my urge for dramatic proclamations.

"It is you who are not worthy to be Archon. You are a disgrace. You are no Master. Only a pretender. You've stolen power from my sister, but it will avail you nothing. Those who dance in shadows have decreed your fall. And her eyes will watch your destruction." I gestured to my sister's double as if inviting her to come forward to testify further against Pavan's inquity.

The tall puppet did not move, but the thin jester who had served the role of doorman stepped from the shadows.

"Do you, Elias Clermont, mean to enter this trial of supremacy against Pavan?"

"I do."

The jester nodded and pulled at the bells of his Fool's Cap as if signaling the start of a prize fight.

Pavan frowned. "On what grounds should I have to waste time with this one?"

The jester grinned and extended an open hand towards me. "Speak the words of invocation, Elias Clermont."

I raised my voice and stroked Virgil's downy horned head. I did not know exactly what was asked for, but we would do our best. "We are practioners of the Old Art and servants of the true order of puppetry. I dedicate my craft along with my loyal Virgil to their Supreme Will. Let it begin with your destruction, Pavan. Perhaps your corpse will serve some use in its elemental parts for junk puppets." I traced an invisible sigil in the air to consecrate the event to the powers I had come here at last to join.

Pavan spat again on the platform and shook his head. "Enough swill from you."

The jester stepped back into the shadows.

Contorting my fingers, the hidden, pierced folds of flesh pulled upon the levers, extending the fangs and claws of Virgil, and the other puppeteers—both those on their stone thrones and those waiting patiently, and perhaps fearfully, for their turns at the trials—stared at the many sharp points that arrayed Virgil's full majesty.

Pavan brandished Gianduja—seamlessly repaired. A slight twist pulled at my belly as Pavan waggled strings that cinched the air between us within an invisible grasp, but with the fibers of my being connecting each day more profoundly to greater unseen powers, I was beyond such paltry methods of clumsy occult compulsion. He lacked the reins of sufficient power to master my mind.

Cursing, Pavan hurled Gianduja against the wall and returned to his more immediate adversary, which had begun to sway, lurching towards Pavan, staring with Sonia's slate gray eyes.

Pavan compelled the mammoth femurs to tremble and stride forth from the walls where they had hung. One of these flipped over and nearly hit me in the face, but I dove and rolled with Virgil, receiving the impact on my flank, so I only sprawled to the floor.

The other huge femur slammed against Sonia's puppet-revenant, and though the kidneys secreted fluid onto the platform, the scarecrow thing appeared unfazed.

Wincing at the bruising of my hip from the flung bone, I regained my feet and gripped Virgil, ready to assist the flesh puppet with Sonja's eyes in the attack on Pavan.

Unlike me, the puppet had not fallen over. It stood in place, though rocking slightly from the assault. The gray eyes of Sonia widened and bulged.

Twirling again the strings he held in his right hand, Pavan lunged forward as though about to lasso some wild animal.

Sure enough, as if he were a wrangler of a stallion, Pavan caught a loop around the throat of the puppet and then drove a pointy-tipped rod into its back.

Then, the puppet wrangled back.

As Pavan more confidently planted his left foot and pulled up another rod, aiming for the other side of the puppet's back, this silent, confident thing with mushy kidneys hidden beneath the folds of leather wrapped round its belly, this leering shape with the slate gray eyes of Sonja, sprang forward. A rainbow of lights from the chromatrope strobed across its swollen pallor.

Virgil and I saw our chance. Any pity for Pavan had vanished in the full flush of rage.

With a cast like that of a fisherman seeking deeper waters, I flicked my hand and tossed Virgil across the room till he soared as does the falcon seeking its finned or furred prey. Rather than seizing pale fish or soft rabbit, Virgil's talons slashed the top of Pavan's head before landing on the back of the tall puppet animated with the organs of Sonja and Yves.

Inspired by the performance of the joining of Geisha and demon puppet, that Sonja had performed at Glanum, Virgil stood atop this hybrid incarnation, a towering totem of wonder.

Pavan pivoted to the side, but he was too late. Virgil bent down with a quick bite of poisoned fangs. As Pavan stiffened into paralytic horror, it was as though a belly-mouthed ogre—one of the squat brainless Blemmyae written of by Herodotus—swayed before him, for beneath the horned crown of Virgil, the seams of the fleshier puppet's mouth parted in a peeling fold that covered Pavan's bald head. The chromatrope's dance of light illuminated speckles of blood.

Sonja's eyes blinked as the puppet's engorged jowls flapped and swelled like a bullfrog calling its patriarchal groaning song out into the depths of the marsh.

I reeled Virgil back to me with a triumphant flourish. Together we watched the shambling simulacrum of Sonja drag the rest of Pavan's exposed, shuddering body behind it as the puppet stalked behind the scarlet screen where the most elite spectators awaited. Whomever had contrived that flesh puppet with Sonja's accusatory eyes did not emerge to take credit for their share of success in this performance.

The thin jester nodded to the robed men and women who conferred on their stone seats. One man in a crimson robe chattered about how "it was the flesh golem, not the boy who won the trial." Others complained about how "he is not one of us, and never can be, for he did not even attend the school!" and stated that "he has yet much to prove."

I saw even in that dim changing light of the chromatope that illuminated the shadows moving across the scarlet screen that these human judges did not look favorably upon me but sought to bar me from glory because of their jealous disdain of my art.

I did not bother at first to engage these pompous and churlish spectators seated above the platform, and I noticed the jester seemed uninterested in their deliberations as well—his waxy smile never changed as he glided over to the same scarlet screen behind which Pavan's abductor had disappeared.

The judges' airs amused Virgil. His manic laughter shivered through me, and my arms trembled with anticipation at what we must finally do.

Those who dance in the shadows, twist without strings and gyre without rods—for the earth is their moving stage—Virgil had whispered to me at night that they were our true audience. I felt now the tremor in the air of their subtle strings. It was their vibrations of primal gnosis I had sensed earlier when Pavan had tried briefly to bridle my will. These numinous tremors now thrilled my nerves and rendered Virgil almost mad with impatience.

And then I saw the leprous whiteness of the jester's face—a mask after all—drift into view from behind the scarlet screen. It fluttered without a body to prop it up, rumpling in the cavern's moist breeze to come to rest like a macabre hand-kerchief on the stone floor.

And so, I saw that the old ways were still true. The gods wait for those who find them. And they had dropped a token of their approval for Virgil and me.

I knew to whom my performance most mattered, but I still wanted to show these arrogant and perverse human puppeteers who sat upon stone thrones who was who and what was what.

"No," I said. "We are not one of you. We will prove why we are better."

While the judges darted glances at each other, I signaled to Virgil that he should gape. His jaw lowered like a portcullis and a flash of fire and puff of smoke emerged. Surely, they would be impressed at clever pyrotechnics.

But no, the Philistine puppeteers watched me unmoved, jaded by their depravity in the trade of organs. Their conjura-tions of baser necromancy than the true Old Art which Virgil and I had renewed.

I even saw the man in crimson shrug. They had lost the capability to appreciate the dexterity of a masterful puppeteer.

The entire crowd of puppeteers barely reacted.

Their disease was a blight of spirit, a sickness of vision.

Such loathsomeness must be purged.

So be it then.

Glaring at them all, this motley group of sinister puppeteers, I began the opening steps of the Dances of both Blood and Delirium, and soon I heard many of them howl around me, as they beat their brows bloody against the pitiless wall.

Then Virgil joined me in the Dance of the Outside. We

watched bright pinpoints of light scatter through the dark of the cave. A radiant illumination that made the chromatrope seem dim.

Some, who must have already been mad or oddly immune, still stared at me, and Virgil, whose copper eyes shone more brightly than ever, took the lead with the strings as he gamboled from body to body, wall-crawling then crouching to lick the blood from the nose or lips or ears of the frenzied victim of his last performance.

And then—for we knew we must do something both older and newer than the lives of these miserable men and women who presumed to make the earth their throne—Virgil and I began our secret masterwork, our tour-de-force of occult puppetry, the Dance of Stone.

The earth shivered beneath my feet, and I swayed comfortably as waves of rippling rock undulated around me. Virgil and I had lisped like lovers of this Dance of Stone in the pitch-black hours of our lonely nights. We had practiced our paces while owls quietly soared beneath the moon. Now we would share in its full performance together in the shadows of this ancient cave.

Virgil's arms spread, his very back impossibly thickening, and his elbows thrust upwards.

Simultaneously, stalagmites pierced up from the floor of the cave, transfixing the few remaining puppeteers. Bleeding to death, they writhed at first like pinned worms while their own puppets swayed and watched their demise..

Then the very minerals of the earth dissolved from their blood and burst from their bones, sprinkling in a fine silvery sand upon the floor. The detritus of the pretenders was swept away by the flapping arms of their remaining puppets.

What had seemed mere subordinate inanimate forms—of cloth and sticks or clay and rods—now delivered in their swaying gaits handfuls of silver dust and chunks of bone to their true artful masters waiting in the darkness behind the scarlet screen.

Flesh had vanished.

Greater things still moved.

A deep murmur followed the silence of this dissolution.

The single word I had waited to hear—"Archon"—hissed from the pulverized dust.

The projecting light from the chromatrope went out.

The shadows were gone, but I could hear the shapes sliding around that scarlet curtain.

I knew we would meet at last. Me and the true masters of occult puppetry.

Truth would not be denied me in this dark.

Now that I had cleared the room of the undeserving, I took up Virgil's perch.

I loosened the strings, and waited for a worthier audience to emerge.

Not mere "puppets," but the true dancing, squirming, shape-shifting masters of rods and strings.

I watched them glide out from the scarlet screen past the waxen white mask of the jester to take their rightful seats on the thrones of ancient stone.

⁓

Acknowledgements

THANKS TO THOMAS LIGOTTI, SUSAN HUBBARD, SEQUOIA Nagamatsu, Robert James Russell, and Andy Duncan for reading and blurbing the manuscript. And a big thanks to all writing teachers I've been able to work with, including my MFA thesis advisor, Lawrence Coates, who pointed out he liked the longer version of this story I was working on during the BGSU MFA program and noting this narrative was a Künstlerroman where the protagonist was perfecting his art. Also, thanks to Wendell Mayo, though he is no longer with us, for his thoughtful remarks. And many thanks to John Dufresne whose craft books and advice has been something I've worked to apply to my own work. A huge thanks to my great friend Chris Aynesworth, who read probably at least three different drafts and shared his impressions of this odyssey of occult puppetry. And many thanks to Eric Bosarge, who plucked this manuscript from the slush pile and gave the puppets a chance to constitute themselves here in print. And lastly a grateful thanks to those who are going to buy and read this book. May you feel something of the dreadful delights that Elias discovers on his journey of artistic and occult mastery.

CPSIA information can be obtained
at www.ICGtesting.com
Printed in the USA
LVHW031601300621
691479LV00009B/1090